Deborah Moggach

TULIP FEVER

VINTAGE

For information on the illustrations, please turn to the back of the book

Published by Vintage 2000

2 4 6 8 10 9 7 5 3 1

First published in Great Britain by William Heinemann in 1999

Vintage
Random House, 20 Vauxhall Bridge Road, London SW1V 2SA

Random House Australia (Pty) Limited
20 Alfred Street, Milsons Point, Sydney,
New South Wales 2061, Australia

Random House New Zealand Limited
18 Poland Road, Glenfield, Auckland 10, New Zealand

Random House South Africa (Pty) Limited
Endulini, 5A Jubilee Road, Parktown 2193, South Africa

The Random House Group Limited Reg. No. 954009
www.randomhouse.co.uk

A CIP catalogue record for this book
is available from the British Library

ISBN 0 09 928885 0

Papers used by Random House are natural, recyclable products made from wood grown in sustainable forests. The manufacturing processes conform to the environmental regulations of the country of origin

Printed and bound in Great Britain by
Cox & Wyman Limited, Reading, Berkshire

This one is for Csaba, again

For their comments and help, my thanks to
Manouk van der Meulen, Russell Hoban,
Wolfgang Ansorge, Judy Cooke, Geraldine Cooke,
Patricia Brent, Periwinkle Unwin, Victoria Salmon,
Jacques Giele, Lee Langley, Sarah Garland,
Alex Hough, Anne Rothenstein, Judy Taylor,
Charlotte Ackroyd, Geraldine Willson-Fraser,
Lottie Moggach, Tom Moggach, and Csaba Pasztor.
The many books I found useful and illuminating
included Simon Schama's *The Embarrassment of Riches*,
Paul Zumthor's *Daily Life in Rembrandt's Holland*,
Mariet Westerman's *A Worldly Art*,
Wayne E. Franit's *Paragons of Virtue*, Bob Haak's
The Golden Age, R. H. Fuchs's *Dutch Painting*,
Michael North's *Art and Commerce in the Dutch Golden
Age*, Paul Taylor's *Dutch Flower Painting 1600–1750* and
Z. Herbert's *Still Life with a Bridle*.

Most of all, my thanks to the Dutch artists themselves,
through whose paintings we step into a lost world,
and find ourselves at home.

It is the people who live on top, restfully and staidly; underneath it is their shadows which move . . . I should not wonder if the surface of the grachts still reflected the shadows of people from bygone centuries, men in broad ruffs and women in mob caps . . . The towns appear to be standing, not on the earth, but on their own reflections; these highly respectable streets appear to emerge from bottomless depths of dreams . . .

Karel Čapek, *Letters from Holland*, 1933

Yes, I knew well the world of poverty and ugliness, but I painted the skin, the glittering surface, the appearance of things: the silky ladies, and gentlemen in irreproachable black. I admired how fiercely they fought for a life slightly longer than the one for which they were destined. They protected themselves with fashion, tailors' accessories, a fancy ruffle, ingenious cuffs . . . any detail that would allow them to last a little longer before they – and we as well – are engulfed by the black background.

Z. Herbert, *Still Life with a Bridle*

Our task is not to solve enigmas, but to be aware of them, to bow our heads before them and also to prepare the eyes for never-ending delight and wonder. If you absolutely require discoveries, however, I will tell you that I am proud to have succeeded in combining a certain particularly intensive cobalt with a luminous lemonlike yellow, as well as recording the reflection of southern light that strikes through thick glass on to a grey wall . . . Allow us to continue our archaic procedure, to tell the world words of reconciliation and to speak of joy from recovered harmony, of the eternal desire for reciprocated love.

Letter attributed to Jan Vermeer

❧ 1 ❧

SOPHIA

Trust not to appearances.

Jacob Cats, *Moral Emblems*, 1632

We are eating dinner, my husband and I. A shred of leek is caught in his beard. I watch it move up and down as he chews; it is like an insect caught in the grass. I watch it idly, for I am a young woman and live simply, in the present. I have not yet died and been reborn. I have not yet died a second time – for in the eyes of the world this will be considered a second death. In my end is my beginning, the eel curls round and swallows its own tail. And in the beginning I am still alive, and young, though my husband is old. We lift our wine flutes and drink. Words are etched on my glass: *Mankind's hopes are fragile glass and life is therefore also short*, a scratched homily through the sinking liquid.

Cornelis tears off a piece of bread and dips it into his soup. He chews for a moment. 'My dear, I have something to discuss.' He wipes his lips with his napkin. 'In this transitory life do we not all crave immortality?'

I freeze, knowing what is coming. I gaze at my roll, lying on the tablecloth. It has split, during baking, and parted like lips. For three years we have been married and I have not produced a child. This is not through lack of trying. My husband is still a vigorous man in this respect. At night he mounts me; he spreads my legs and

I

I lie there like an upturned beetle pressed down by a shoe. With all his heart he longs for a son – an heir to skip across these marble floors and give a future to this large, echoing house on the Herengracht.

So far I have failed him. I submit to his embraces, of course, for I am a dutiful wife and shall always be grateful to him. The world is treacherous and he reclaimed me, as we reclaimed our country from the sea, draining her and ringing her with dykes to keep her safe, to keep her from going under. I love him for this.

And then he surprises me. 'To this effect I have engaged the services of a painter. His name is Jan van Loos and he is one of the most promising artists in Amsterdam – still lifes, landscapes, but most especially portraiture. He comes on the recommendation of Hendrick Uylenburgh, who as you know is a discerning dealer – Rembrandt van Rijn, newly arrived from Leiden, is one of his protégés.'

My husband lectures me like this. He tells me more than I want to know but tonight his words land noiselessly around me.

Our portrait is going to be painted! 'He is thirty-six, the same age as our brave new century.' Cornelis drains his glass and pours another. He is drunk with the vision of ourselves, immortalized on canvas. Drinking beer sends him to sleep, but drinking wine makes him patriotic. 'Ourselves, living in the greatest city, home to the greatest nation on the globe.' It is only me sitting opposite him but he addresses a larger audience. Above his yellowed beard his cheeks are flushed. 'For doesn't Vondel describe Amsterdam thus? *What waters are not shadowed by her sails? On which mart does she not sell her wares? What peoples does she not see lit by the moon, she who herself sets the laws of the whole ocean?'*

He does not expect an answer for I am just a young wife, with little life beyond these walls. Around my waist hang keys to nothing but our linen chests, for I have yet to unlock anything of more significance. In fact, I am wondering what clothes I shall wear for my portrait. That is the size of my world so far. Forget oceans and empires.

Maria brings in a plate of herrings and retreats, sniffing. Fog rolls in off the sea and she has been coughing all day. This hasn't dampened her spirits. I am sure she has a secret lover; she hums in the kitchen and sometimes I catch her standing in front of a mirror rearranging her hair under her cap. I shall find out. We are confidantes, or as much confidantes as our circumstances allow. Since I left my sisters she is the only one I have.

Next week the painter will arrive. My husband is a connoisseur of paintings, our house is filled with them. Behind him, on the wall, hangs a canvas of *Susannah and the Elders*. The old men peer at the naked girl as she bathes. By daylight I can see their greedy faces but now, in the candle-light, they have retreated back into the shadows; all I can see is her plump, pale flesh above my husband's head. He lifts a fish on to his plate. He is a collector of beautiful things.

I see us as a painting. Cornelis, his white lace collar against black, his beard moving as he eats. The herring lying on my plate, its glistening, scored skin split open to reveal the flesh within; the parted lips of my roll. Grapes, plump and opaque in the candle-light; the pewter goblet glowing dully.

I see us there, sitting at our dining-table, motionless – our own frozen moment before everything changes.

After dinner he reads to me from the Bible. '*All flesh is grass, and all the goodliness thereof is as the flower of the field; the grass withereth, the flower fadeth, because the spirit of the Lord bloweth upon it; surely the people is grass . . .*'

But I am already hanging on the wall, watching us.

2

MARIA

She must have a diligent eye to the behaviour of her servants, what meetings and greetings, what ticklings and toyings, and what words and countenances there be betweene men and maides, lest such matters being neglected, there follow wantonness, yea folly, within their houses, which is a great blemish to the governours.

J. Dod and R. Cleaver, *A Godly Forme of Household Government*, 1612

Maria the maid, dozy with love, polishes the copper warming pan. She is heavy with desire; she feels sluggish, as if she is moving around underwater. Her face, distorted by the curved metal, smiles back at herself. She is a big, ruddy country girl with a healthy appetite. Her conscience, too, is a healthily adaptable organ. When she takes Willem into her bed, deep in the wall behind the kitchen fire, she pulls the curtain to shut out God's disapproval. Out of sight, out of mind. After all, she and Willem will some day be married.

She dreams about this. She dreams that the master and mistress have died – shipwrecked at sea – and that she and Willem live in this house with their six sweet children. When she is cleaning, she cleans for his homecoming. When her mistress is out she closes the bottom half of the window shutters so that she cannot be seen from the street. The parlour is thrown into shadow, as if she is walking on the sea bed. She puts on her mistress's blue velvet jacket, trimmed with fur collar and cuffs, and she walks around the house casually catching sight of herself in the mirrors. It is a simple dream; where is the harm in it?

Maria is in the parlour now, on her knees. She is scrubbing the blue-and-white tiles around the skirting. Each tile shows a child playing – one with a hoop, one with a ball. One, her favourite, rides a hobby-horse. The room is lined with her imaginary children. She wipes them tenderly with a cloth.

Through the wall she hears the noises in the street – footsteps, voices. Bred in the country, she is still surprised by the bustle of the Herengracht, by how close the street presses in against her secret world indoors. The flower seller cries out, his voice as eerie as a peewit. The man from the pewter foundry rattles his tin, calling vessels out to be repaired as if he were summoning sinners. Somebody, startlingly close, hawks and spits.

And then she hears his bell. 'Fish, fresh fish!' Willem sings tunelessly; he has a terrible voice. 'Roach–bream–herrings–cod!' Then he rings his bell. She is as alert as a shepherdess to the ding-dong of her darling in the midst of the flock.

Maria jumps up. She wipes her nose on her apron, smooths down her skirt and pulls open the door. It is a foggy morning; she can barely see the canal beyond the pavement. Willem looms out of the mist. 'Hello, my lovely.' His face splits into a smile.

'What've you got there?' she says. 'Give us a look.'

'What do you want, Maria my duck?' He shifts the basket on to his hip.

'How about a nice fat eel?'

'How do you like it?'

'You know how I like it,' she chuckles.

'How about stewed with apricots and sweet vinegar?'

'Mm.' She sighs. Down the road she hears barrels being unloaded from a barge. They fall on to the street, *thump-thump*, the thump of her heart.

'How about a herring?' he asks. 'How about a kiss?'

He moves up the step, closer to her. *Thump-thump*.

'Ssh!' She backs away. People are passing. Willem hangs his head dolefully. He is a plain man – long, lugubrious, rubbery face, the sort of face that causes merriment in others. She loves it when it breaks into a smile. He is a darling, innocent man and he makes her feel worldly wise. Her! That is how innocent he is.

Willem cannot believe she loves him. 'I came by yesterday. Why didn't you open the door?'

'Oh, the vegetable man was showing me his carrots.'

'You teasing me?'

'I was at the market.' She smiles at him. 'It's you I love. I'm like a mussel, closed in my shell. It's only you who can open me.'

She steps back and lets him into the house. He dumps down his basket and flings his arms around her.

'Ugh! Your fingers!' She leads him through the *voorhuis*, along the passageway, down the steps into the kitchen. He pinches her bottom as they stumble across to the sink.

She yanks the lever. Water gushes out of the tap, on to his outstretched hands. He stands there, as obedient as a child with its mother. She rubs his fingers dry and then she sniffs them. He presses his body against hers; he presses his knee between her thighs – she nearly swoons – and kisses her.

'You can't stay long,' she whispers. 'They're both at home.'

She pulls him with her, into her bed in the wall. They fall over the wooden rim and collapse, laughing, on the mattress. How warm it is in here; the warmest bed in the place. When they own the house they will still sleep down here because it is her burrow, the hub of her existence.

He breathes sweet words into her ear. She tickles him. He yelps. She shushes him. She takes his hand and pushes it up between her legs; they've no time to lose. They giggle like children for they have both grown up sleeping squashed against their brothers and sisters, snuggling and squirming and knocking knees.

'Now what's down here?' she whispers. 'Anything interesting?'

Far off there's a *rat-a-tat-tat* on the front door.

Maria jerks upright. She pushes Willem off and struggles out of bed.

A moment later, flushed and breathless, she unlatches the front door.

A man stands there. He is short and dark – shiny black curls, blue eyes and a velvet beret on his head. 'I have an appointment,' he says. 'I have come to paint a portrait.'

❧ 3 ❧

SOPHIA

The ripe pear falls ready to the hand.

Jacob Cats, *Moral Emblems*, 1632

'My hand should be here, on my hip?' Cornelis half turns towards the painter. His chest is thrust out and his other hand grasps his cane. He wears his brocade coat and black stovepipe hat; he has combed his beard and waxed his moustache into points. Today he wears a ruff – deep and snowy white. It detaches his head from his body, as if it is being served on a platter. He is trying to conceal his excitement.

'You know the proverb, *you cannot dam a stream for the water gushes forth elsewhere*? Though we have whitewashed our churches, banning holy images from within them –' He inclines his head in my direction. 'Here I must beg my wife's pardon, for she is a Catholic – though our Reformed church has withdrawn its patronage from painters, their talent has bubbled up elsewhere and we are the beneficiaries, for they paint our daily life with a luminosity and loving attention to detail that – without being blasphemous – can border on the transcendental.'

The painter catches my eye. He raises his eyebrows and smiles. How dare he! I look away.

'Madam, please keep your head still,' he says.

We are being painted in my husband's library. The curtain is pulled back; sunlight streams into the room. It shines on to his cabinet of curiosities – fossils, figurines, a nautilus shell mounted on a silver plinth. The table, draped with a Turkey rug, carries a globe of the world, a pair of scales and a human skull. The globe represents my husband's trade, for he is a merchant. He owns a warehouse in the harbour; he imports grain from the Baltic and rare spices from the Orient. He sends shiploads of textiles to countries that are way beyond my small horizon. He is proud to display his wealth but also, like a good Calvinist, humbled by the transience of earthly riches – hence the scales, for the weighing of our sins on the Day of Judgment; hence the skull. *Vanity, vanity, all is vanity*. He wanted to rest his hand on the skull, but the painter has rearranged him.

Cornelis is talking. In the corner of my eye I see his beard moving up and down, like a yellow furry animal, on his ruff. I urge him silently to stop. 'I am fortunate that, through my endeavours, I have reached a position of means and rank.' He clears his throat. 'I am most fortunate, however, in possessing a jewel beside which rubies lose their lustre – I mean my dear Sophia. For a man's greatest joy and comfort is a happy home, where he can close the door after his day's labours and find peace and solace beside the fireplace, enjoying the loving attentions of a blessed wife.'

A muffled snicker. The painter stifles his mirth. Behind his easel he is looking at me again; I can feel his eyes, though my own are fixed on the wall. I hate him.

Worse is to come. 'My only sadness is that, as yet, we have not heard the patter of tiny feet, but that I hope will be rectified.' My husband chuckles. 'For though my leaves may be sere, the sap still rises.'

No! How could he say this? The painter catches my eye again. He grins – white teeth. He looks me up and down, disrobing me. My dress vanishes and I stand in front of him, naked.

I want to die. My whole body is blushing. Why are we doing this? How could Cornelis talk this way? It is his excitement at having his portrait painted – but how could he make us such fools?

Behind his easel the painter is watching me. His blue eyes bore into my soul. He is a small, wiry man with wild black hair. His head is cocked to one side. I stare back at him coolly. Then I realize – he is not looking at *me*. He is looking at an arrangement to be painted. He wipes his brush on a rag and frowns. I am just an object – brown hair, white lace collar and blue, shot-silk dress.

This irritates me. I am not a joint of mutton! My heart thumps; I feel dizzy and confused. What is the matter with me?

'How long is this going to take?' I ask coldly.

'You're already tired?' The painter steps up to me and gives me a handkerchief. 'Are you unwell?'

'I'm perfectly well.'

'You've been sniffing all morning.'

'It's just a chill. I caught it from my maid.' I won't use his handkerchief. I pull out my own and dab at my nose. He moves close to me; I can smell linseed oil and tobacco.

'You're not happy, are you?' he asks.

'What do you mean, sir?'

'I mean – you're not happy, standing.' He pulls up a chair. 'Sit here. If I move this . . . and this . . .' He shifts the table. He moves quickly, rearranging the furniture.

He puts the globe to one side and stands back, inspecting it. He works with utter concentration. His brown jerkin is streaked with paint.

And then he is squatting in front of me. He tweaks the hem of my dress, revealing the toe of my slipper. He pulls off his beret and scratches his head. I look down at his curls. He sits back on his haunches, looks at my foot and then reaches forth and cradles it in his hand. He moves it a little to the right and, placing it on the footwarmer, adjusts the folds of my skirt. 'A woman like you deserves to be happy,' he murmurs.

He steps back behind his easel. He says he will visit for three sittings and complete the canvas in his studio. My husband is talking now, telling him about a man he knows, a friend of the Burgomaster, who lost a ship at sea and with it a great fortune, sunk by the Spanish. Cornelis's voice echoes, far away. I sit there. My breasts press against the cotton of my chemise; my thighs burn under my petticoat. I am conscious of my throat, my earlobes, my pulsing blood. My body is throbbing but this is because I have a fever. This is why I am aching, why I am both heavy and feather-light.

The painter works. His eyes flick to me and back to his canvas. As he paints I feel his brush stroking my skin . . .

I am in bed with my sisters. I keep my eyes squeezed shut because I know he's sitting there, watching me. His red tongue flicks over his teeth. If I open my eyes the wolf will be there, sitting on his haunches beside my bed. My heart squeezes. I mutter my rosary . . . *Hail Mary, Mother of God* . . . I can feel his hot, meaty breath on my face. My hands cup my budding breasts. I mutter faster, willing him to move closer.

❧ 4 ❧

MARIA

My duty requires me to work but Love will not allow me
*   any rest.*
I do not feel like doing anything;
My thoughts are nourished by Love, Love nourishes my
*   thoughts,*
And when I fight it, I am powerless.
Everything I do is against my will and desire
Because you, o restless Love, hold me in your Power!

                                        J. H. Krul, 1644

'I love him. When he touches me I get these shivers all over my body. When he looks at me it turns my insides to jelly.' Maria leans against the linen cupboard, her eyes closed. 'I'm so happy I'm going to burst. Oh, madam, I'll love him for ever and ever and we're going to have six children because I ate an apple this morning, the same time as I was thinking about him, and when I spat out the pips there were six of them.'

Maria clasps the sheet to her breasts. She did not mean to confess it but the words surged up. She has nobody to tell except her mistress; she is her only confidante for Maria knows nobody in Amsterdam except tradespeople and her darling sweetheart, her doleful, fond, funny Willem with his fishy fingers.

'I love him to death.'

Sophia does not reply. She takes the sheets from

Maria's arms and loads them into the cupboard. The cat rubs himself against Sophia's legs. Getting no reaction, he stalks stiff-legged to Maria and rubs himself against hers. He moves from one woman to the other, seeking a response, but they are far away in their own dreams.

Both women sneeze at the same time. Maria laughs at this, but Sophia seems not to notice. This annoys the maid who had expected some eager questions from her mistress. *Who is he? When did you meet him? Are his intentions honourable?* (Yes.)

Outside, the light is fading. Sophia closes the cupboard door and leans against it. She looks like a doll, propped up. She wears the blue silk dress she wore this morning, for the sitting, but she has now hung her gold crucifix around her neck. She looks pale; this is no doubt because she is feeling unwell although she refuses to go to bed. Maria thinks she is very pretty, in a refined sort of way. Beside her, Maria feels like a lump of dough. Today her mistress resembles a piece of china that might break.

Maria is not a curious woman and her happiness has made her self-absorbed. She knows little about her mistress except that they are of the same age – twenty-four – and that Sophia's father, who worked as a printer in Utrecht, died young leaving heavy debts and several daughters. That is why Sophia was married off to a rich man. Maria thinks that Cornelis is an old bore, but she is a practical woman. One has to survive and there is always a price to pay for this. Theirs is a trading nation, the most spectacularly successful the world has ever seen, and a transaction has been made between her mistress and her master. Youth has been traded for wealth; fertility (possible fertility) has been exchanged for a life free from the terrors of starvation. To Maria it seems a sensible arrangement, for though she is dreamy and superstitious she is a peasant at heart and has her feet planted firmly on the ground.

Still, she is irritated. She has opened up her heart and for what? Silence. Carrying an armful of sheets she stomps into the bedchamber. Her mistress follows her in to help make up the bed – they often work together. On the oak chest three candles are burning. Maria dumps the sheets on the bed and blows one out.

'Why are you doing that?' asks Sophia.

Maria shivers. 'Three candles are a bad omen.'

'What omen?'

'Death,' she replies shortly. 'Don't you know?'

❦ 5 ❧

CORNELIS

*Of the Poses of Women and Girls: In women and girls
there must be no actions where the legs are raised or too far
apart, because that would indicate boldness and a general
lack of shame, while legs closed together indicate the fear of
disgrace.*

Leonardo da Vinci, *Notebooks*

'Fish again?' Cornelis looks at the plate. 'All this week
we have eaten fish. Last week too, if I remember rightly.
Soon we will be sprouting fins.' He chuckles at his own
joke. 'Much of our country once lay underwater – are you
returning us to that element?'

'Sir,' says the maid, 'I thought you liked fish. This is
bream, your favourite.' She indicates Sophia. 'She's
prepared it with prunes, the way you prefer it.'

He turns to his wife. 'How about a nice piece of pork?
Visit the butcher tomorrow, my love, before we are all
transformed into the scaly denizens of the deep.'

Maria snorts – with laughter or contempt, he cannot
tell – and goes back to the kitchen. The impertinence!
Since Karel, the manservant, left, standards have been
slipping; Cornelis must talk to his wife about it.

Sophia does not eat. She looks at her wineglass and
says: 'I don't want that painter back in the house.'

'What did you say?'

'I don't want him here. I don't want us to have our portrait painted.'

He stares at her. 'But why not?'

'Please!'

'But why?'

'It's dangerous,' she says.

'Dangerous?'

She pauses. 'We are just – pandering to our own vanity.'

'So what are you pandering to, my love, when the dressmaker visits?'

'That's not the same –'

'How many hours do you spend on fittings, twisting this way and that in front of the mirror?' He leans across the table and strokes her wrist. 'I am glad you do, my sweetheart, for it fills my old heart with joy to see your beauty. That is the reason I want to preserve that bloom on canvas – do you understand?'

She fiddles with the hem of the table-cloth. 'It's too expensive. Eighty florins!'

'Cannot I spend my money how I choose?'

'Eighty florins is many months' wages for – say – a carpenter . . .' She falters. 'A sailor.'

'Why is this suddenly a concern of yours?'

There is another silence. Then she says: 'I don't like him.'

'He seems a pleasant enough fellow.'

She looks up, her face pink. 'I don't like him – he's impudent.'

'If you truly dislike like the man – why, I'll pay him off and find another.' Cornelis wants to please her. 'There's Nicholaes Eliasz or Thomas de Keyser. They have many commissions, we might have to bear with a delay. I could even approach Rembrandt van Rijn, though the prices he charges might stretch even my means.' He smiles at her. 'Anything to make you happy, my dearest heart.'

Relieved, he eats. So that was all it was. Women are strange creatures with such funny little ways. How tricky they are, compared with men. They are like a puzzle box – you have to twist a dial here, turn a key there, and only then will you unlock their secrets.

Cornelis loves his wife to distraction. Sometimes, caught in the candle-light, her beauty stops his heart. She is his hope, his joy, the spring in his step. She is a miracle, for she has brought him back to life when he had given up hope. She rescued him, just as he himself, in another way entirely, rescued her.

After dinner Cornelis puts another slab of peat on the fire, sits down and lights his pipe. *A man's greatest comfort is a happy home, where he can enjoy the attentions of a loving wife.* Sophia, however, is absent. Her footsteps creak across the ceiling. Then there is silence. She said she had a headache and retired early. Usually she sits with him and sews; sometimes they play cards together. Tonight she has been restless, as jumpy as a mare sensing a thunderstorm. That outburst about the painter was most uncharacteristic.

Cornelis worries that she is falling ill; she looked pale this evening. Maybe she is missing her family. She has few friends here in Amsterdam and the wives of his own acquaintances are a great deal older than she is. She does not go out enough, she does not enjoy herself. When they were first betrothed Sophia was a lively, happy girl but over the months she has grown more withdrawn.

Maybe it is caused by the responsibilities of running this household – they must employ another servant. Perhaps his wife feels trapped in this house, like the goldfinch he kept in a cage when he was a boy.

Cornelis knocks out his pipe and gets to his feet. His joints ache; his back hurts. It has been a long winter. He feels the weight of the fog outside, weighing down on the city like the lid of a *hutspot* cauldron. He feels his age.

He locks up. He blows out the candles, all except one, which he carries upstairs. The smell of cooked fish still lingers in the house. Yesterday a whale was washed up on the beach at Beverwijk. It was a huge creature, the largest ever measured in that area. The local people were thrown into turmoil. It was an unnatural omen, a portent of disaster – a monster vomited up by the ocean to punish them for their sins.

Cornelis is aware that this is simple-minded. He knows this from his own experience. Tragedy does not take its cue from nature's eruptions; it strikes at random. No shattering mirror caused the death of his first dear wife Hendrijke, when she was barely forty. No conjunction of the stars caused his two babies to die in infancy.

For Cornelis has already lost one family. Like all the bereaved, he knows that the world is senseless. They know this in their hearts, even though they tell others, and themselves, that it is God's will. He performs his pious duty. Each night he reads to Sophia from the Bible; they bow their heads in prayer. On Sunday he visits his church and she attends a secret Mass, for her religion is tolerated as long as it is celebrated in private. He feels, however, that he is mouthing the words like a fish. His world offers no vocabulary for doubt. He has not admitted it in so many words to himself. All he knows is that loss has weakened rather than reinforced his faith and the only sure thing to which he can cling lies here in his feather bed.

Cornelis enters the bedchamber. Sophia is kneeling in prayer. This surprises him; he thought she was already in bed. She must have been praying for some time. When she sees him she starts. She crosses herself and climbs up into the bed where she lies staring at the ceiling. From the beam hangs her paper bridal coronet, dusty now, like a wasps' nest.

Deep in the bed she sighs and shifts. She exhales the fragrance of youth. Desire warms his old bones; it spreads through his cold, sluggish bloodstream. He undresses, empties his bladder into the chamberpot and pulls on his nightshirt. This bed is his life-raft; each night her firm young arms save him from drowning.

Sophia lies curled up, her head buried in the pillows. She is pretending to sleep. He blows out the candle and climbs into bed. He pulls up her shift and cups her small breast in his hand. He kneads the nipple. 'My dear wife,' he whispers. He guides her hand down to his shrunken member. 'My little soldier's dozy tonight. Time to report for duty.'

Her fingers are clenched. He uncurls them and places them around his flesh; he moves her hand up and down. 'Time for battle . . .' His member stiffens; his breathing grows hoarse. 'Stand to attention, sir,' he mutters; it is a little joke he shares with his wife. Opening her legs, he eases himself into position. She shudders, briefly, as he pushes himself in. Burying his face in her hair, he cups her buttocks in his hands and presses her against him as the bedsprings creak rhythmically. His breathing quickens as he slides in and out.

Minutes pass. As he grows older it takes longer to spill his seed. When he is flagging he remembers an incident from his past; its wickedness never fails to inflame him. He is a boy back in Antwerp and the family maidservant, Grietje, comes to say good-night. Suddenly she lifts her skirts and puts his hand between her legs. He feels wiry hair and damp lips. She moves his fingers; the lips slide together like thick slices of beef. She pushes his finger against what feels like a marble, hidden in the slippery folds of her flesh; she makes him rub it . . . up and down, harder and harder . . . Suddenly her thighs clamp together, trapping his hand. She groans. Then she pulls out his hand, laughs, slaps his face and leaves.

At the time he was frightened. Terrified, in fact. Disgusted and ashamed. He was only ten years old. His damp fingers smelt of brine, and a faint aroma of rotting melons. Remembering it, however, works its magic. He trembles at his own wickedness – ah, but it excites him too. 'It's coming . . . it's coming . . . fire the cannons!' he whispers and suddenly he is pumping his seed inside her. He grips her flesh in a final spasm; his thin shanks shiver. And then he collapses, spent, his old heart hammering against his ribs. 'Praise be to God,' he pants.

Sophia lies beneath him without stirring. She seems to be speaking. He can hear her voice but not the words, his heart is pounding in his ears.

'What did you say, my love?'

'I said, I have changed my mind.' She turns her face from his and buries it in the pillow. 'What I told you at dinner . . . I have changed my mind. I don't want another painter.' She pauses. 'Let that man come back.'

6

MARIA

Stolen waters are sweet, and bread eaten in secret places is pleasant.

Jacob Cats, *Moral Emblems*, 1632

Down below, in her bed in the wall, Maria sleeps. On the floor she has laid her shoes upside down to keep away the witches. Outside, the canal exhales its chill breath into the air.

The fog has cleared. The moon slides out from behind a cloud and shines on the rows of houses that line the Herengracht. They are rich people's houses, built to last; their brick gables rear into the sky. Sightlessly, their windows shine in the moonlight. Between them lies the canal. A breeze ruffles the water; it creases like satin. Far away a dog barks – first one and then another, spreading like news of the outbreak of war, a war that only the dogs know is approaching.

The nightwatchman tramps through the streets. He blows his horn, announcing the hour, but Maria snores in the childless house. She dreams that the rooms fill up with water and her master and mistress, locked in their curtained bed, float away. The sea rises and submerges the city but now she is a fish swimming through the rooms. Look, I can breathe! She is free while all the others drown – all but her babies. A flickering shoal, they swim behind her. They dart here and there, suspended above the chequer-board marble floors.

Maria smiles, mistress of her underwater palace. Others have died so that she can live, and in the world of dreams this seems perfectly fitting.

❦§ 7 §❧

CORNELIS

If the poet says that he can inflame men with love, which is
the central aim in all animal species, the painter has the
power to do the same, and to an even greater degree, in that
he can place in front of the lover the true likeness of that
which is beloved, often making him kiss and speak to it.

Leonardo da Vinci, Notebooks

Two weeks pass before the next sitting. Cornelis is a
busy man, he is always out and about. He has his
warehouse to run, down in the harbour. At midday the
Stock Market opens and he hurries down to the Bourse.
Amsterdam is awash with capital and dealing there is
brisk, often frenzied, because the place closes at two. In
addition to this he has civic duties for he is a prominent
citizen, a man of substance in this burgeoning city. It is
1636 and Amsterdam is thriving. The seat of government is in The Hague, but Amsterdam is the true capital
of the Republic. Trade is booming; the arts are
flourishing. Fashionable men and woman stroll along its
streets and the canals mirror back the handsome houses
in which they live. The city is threaded with mirrors.
They reflect the cold spring sunshine. Copper-coloured
clouds lie motionless beneath the bridges. The city sees
itself in its own water like a woman gazing into a
looking-glass. Can we not forgive vanity in one so
beautiful?

And hanging in a thousand homes, paintings mirror back the lives that are lived there. A woman plays the virginal; she catches the eye of the man beside her. A handsome young soldier lifts a glass to his lips; his reflection shines in the silver-topped decanter. A maid gives her mistress a letter . . . The mirrored moments are stilled, suspended in aspic. For centuries to come people will gaze at these paintings and wonder what is about to happen. That letter, what does it say to the woman who stands at the window, the sunlight streaming on to her face? Is she in love? Will she throw away the letter or will she obey it, waiting until the house is empty and stealing out through the rooms that recede, bathed in shafts of sunshine, at the back of the painting?

Who can tell? For her face is serene, her secrets locked into her heart. She stands there, trapped in her frame, poised at a moment of truth. She has yet to make her decision.

Sophia stands at a window. She has not seen Cornelis approach. She is standing half-way up the stairs. The window-panes are tinted glass – amber and blood-red. In the centre is painted a bird trapped in foliage. She cannot see out. The sun shines through, suffusing her face with colour. She stands there, utterly still.

Cornelis thinks: she is already a painting – here, now, before she has been immortalized on canvas. Then he feels an odd sensation. His wife has vanished, her soul sucked away, and just her outward form remains in its cobalt-blue dress.

'My love –' he says.

She jumps, and swings round.

'Did you not hear the knock at the door? Mr van Loos is here, he is waiting downstairs.'

Her hand flies to her hair. 'He's here?'

Cornelis has placed a vase of tulips on the table. He has asked for it to be included in the painting for tulips are a passion of his.

'I bought these at some expense,' he says. 'They are *tulipa clusiana*, forced under glass. That is why we can enjoy them at this early season. They were grown by the Portuguese Jew Francisco Gomez da Costa.' The white petals are flushed with pink. 'It is no wonder, is it, that a poet compared them with the faint blush on the cheek of chaste Susannah?' He clears his throat. 'Do they not remind us of the transitory nature of beauty, how that which is lovely must one day die?'

'Perhaps that's why we should grasp it while we can,' says the painter.

There is a silence. Sophia shifts in her seat.

'I hardly think you would find *that* teaching in our Scriptures.' Cornelis clears his throat again. Painters are known to be godless, disreputable fellows. 'Besides, I have found my heaven on earth.' Cornelis feels a rush of love for his wife. He leans down and touches her cheek.

'Don't move!' says the painter sharply. 'Return to your position please.'

Cornelis, stung, puts his hand back on his hip. Sometimes he gets carried away and forgets that he is having his portrait painted. But it is hard work. Standing upright makes his back ache.

Jan van Loos stands behind his easel. He paints

noiselessly. The sound of brushing comes from the next room, where Maria is sweeping the floor.

'Is it not strange, this madness that has gripped us?' asks Cornelis.

'What madness?' asks the painter.

'Have you surrendered to this passion yet?'

The painter pauses. 'It depends what passion you are talking about.'

'This speculation on tulip bulbs.'

'Ah.' The painter smiles. 'Tulip bulbs.'

Beside Cornelis, his wife shifts in her seat again. Cornelis decides that this painter is somewhat slow-witted. 'I thought we were a sober people,' he says, 'but over the past two years we have become a nation possessed.'

'So I have heard.'

'And it has enslaved people from all ranks – turf cutters and barge skippers, butchers and bakers. Maybe painters too.'

'Not me,' replies the painter. 'I know nothing of business.'

'Ah, nor do they. But great fortunes have been made and lost. These new hybrids that they have been growing – they fetch the most astonishing prices. Thousands of florins, if you know when to buy and sell.' Cornelis's voice rises with excitement; he too has greatly profited from this tulipomania. 'Why, one Semper Augustus bulb – they are the most beautiful and the most valuable – one bulb was sold last week for six fine horses, three oxheads of wine, a dozen sheep, two dozen silver goblets and a seascape by Esaias van de Velde!'

The painter raises his eyebrows and carries on

working. A petal drops, like a shed skirt, from one of the tulips. It lies on the table. Sweep ... sweep ... goes Maria's broom. They can hear her humming.

There is a drowsy, drugged atmosphere in the room. Cornelis suddenly feels alone, as if he is travelling in a coach and everyone else has fallen asleep. Why doesn't his wife respond?

'It is not a native plant, of course – it comes from Turkey. When I was a young man the tulip was known only to the *cognoscenti* – aristocrats and horticulturalists. But we are a green-fingered, resourceful people, are we not? And, nourished by our rich soil the humble bulb has been developed into ever-richer and more spectacular varieties. No wonder people have been losing grip of their senses, for even in death a tulip is beautiful. Your own colleagues have immortalized them on canvas – the Bosschaert brothers, Jan Davidsz de Heem – pictures of astonishing realism which, unlike the flowers they depict, will continue to bloom for generations to come –'

'Please stop talking,' says Jan. 'I'm trying to paint your mouth.'

Sophia makes a snuffling sound. She is laughing. She stops, quickly.

Cornelis's skin stings, as if he has been slapped. Where is the respect? He has so much to teach his wife, so many years of experience in the world. Sometimes he suspects that her attention is wandering. She is so young – such a pretty creature but her head is full of nonsense. He suddenly misses his first wife Hendrijke. How solid and reliable she was. Hendrijke never set his blood on fire, he never felt for her what he feels for Sophia, but she was a true companion. Sophia is so moody – one minute loving, the next distracted and skittish. For the past few days she has been acting quite strangely.

He sets his face in a stern expression. He puffs out his chest and grips his cane. He is not entirely sure that he likes this fellow. Sophia herself had voiced her doubts. But they have started; they had better go through with it.

❧ 8 ❧

THE PAINTING

How may paintings have preserved the image of a divine beauty which in its natural manifestation has been rapidly overtaken by time or death. Thus, the work of the painter is nobler than that of nature, its mistress.

Leonardo da Vinci

Jan van Loos is not painting the old man's mouth. He is painting Sophia's lips. He mixes pink on his palette – ochre, grey and carmine – and strokes the paint lovingly on the canvas. She is gazing at him. For a moment, when the old man was talking, her lips curved into a smile – a smile of complicity. He paints the ghost of this, though it is now gone.

There is no sound in the house. The painting, when it is finished, will look the most tranquil of scenes. Downstairs, Maria has fallen asleep. Exhausted by love she snoozes on a chair in the kitchen. Willem crept into her bed, the night before, and crept out at dawn. As she sleeps the tom-cat drags a plaice across the floor. He too does this noiselessly. This small theft is detected by nobody.

Upstairs, something else is being stolen. Cornelis, too, is drowsy. Sunshine pours through the library window. There is a stone chimney-piece here, supported by caryatids. The sun bathes their breasts. The fossils wait, through centuries of waiting.

Half an hour passes. The painter has scarcely touched his canvas. He is gazing at Sophia. Behind her, on the wall, hangs a *Descent from the Cross*. It is an Italian painting, by the school of Caravaggio. Christ is being lowered. Light illuminates his naked torso. He is no pale, passive, Northern Christ. He is a real man – broad shoulders, muscles, ropes of veins. He has suffered and been slaughtered. The weight of him, upended, fills the frame. He seems to be sliding down on the heads of the couple below.

Beneath Christ stands the old man, the patriarch, his chest thrust out above his spindly legs. His face, cushioned by his ruff, dares the viewer to question his fitness as one of God's chosen. Beside him sits his beautiful young wife. Her hair is pulled back demurely from her face but pearls glint within it, winking at the viewer. They tell a different story. On her lips there is the faintest smile. For whom is she smiling, the painter or the viewer? And is it really a smile at all?

Cornelis is talking but nobody listens. Sophia and the painter gaze at each other with a terrible seriousness. Another petal falls; it reveals the firm knob of the stigma.

Jan starts to paint. The disrobed tulip, in the painting, will be back in full bloom. Centuries later people will stand in the Rijksmuseum and gaze at this canvas. What will they see? Tranquillity, harmony. A married couple who, though surrounded by wealth, are aware that this life is swiftly over (the scales, the skull). Maybe the old man was talking, but he is silent now. They didn't listen then and now nobody can hear.

His young wife is indeed beautiful. Her gaze is candid and full of love. The blush remains in her cheek but she has perished, long ago. Only the painting remains.

ᴥ 9 ᴥ

SOPHIA

I saw the green parrot hanging in the parlour.
Although he was caged, he spoke beautifully . . .
And he was so cheerful in his prison, as if in a wedding
*   house . . .*
If I may be your slave, take me, in slavery,
Tie my hand to your hand, let the wedding ring be the
*   band.*

Van der Minnen, 1694

I am walking with my maid down the Street of Knives. It
is a bright, blustery morning. Outside the shops the
blades glint in the sun, as if soldiers are standing to
attention. *My little soldier's dozy tonight . . .* I squeeze my
eyes shut.

'You've never played Head in Lap?' Maria asks me.

I open my eyes. 'What's that?'

'One boy chooses a girl and buries his head in her lap.
The others take turns smacking his bottom and he has to
guess who they are.' She chuckles. 'And the more they
smack, the deeper goes his head.'

It rained in the night; the buildings look rinsed. High
above us a maid leans out of a window and shakes a
duster. We are going to the market. We walk down the
Street of Cakes, sighing at the smell. A man raises his hat
and smiles.

'Do you know him?' asks Maria.

'Do you?'

'Smack his bottom and see if he guesses.'

We giggle. Sometimes, when we go shopping to-gether, I feel like a girl again with my sisters. I feel released from that great chilly house. However much you bank up the fires, it is impossible to warm the rooms.

If I may be your slave, take me, in slavery. The ruination of my family cut short my youth. My girlish dreams evaporated in the cruel climate of our straitened circumstances. Of course I felt affection for Cornelis, and gratitude; I am ashamed to admit, at the time, that I was also glad to escape the miseries of my life at home. But recently I feel that I have exchanged one kind of imprisonment for another.

It is March; spring has arrived. Maria and I walk under a horse-chestnut tree. Its sticky buds have split apart; the packaged leaves spill out. Their tender green stabs my heart. Approaching the square, we hear the murmur of the market. At first it is faint, like the sea. As we walk nearer it grows into a roar – the stall holders shouting out their wares, the clatter of carts. My spirits rise.

A one-legged man swings past us on his crutches. He grins at us and licks his lips. Maria laughs. 'Hello, peg-leg, missed your dinner?'

'Maria!' I pull her along.

She laughs; she doesn't care. Today she looks shameless. Her bodice is unlaced, revealing the freckled curve of her breasts. I ought to admonish her. I ought to quote her the proverb about wantonness: *If you peel an onion you produce tears.* Yet I envy her – how I envy her! She is free, she is young – far younger than I feel. Next to me she seems like a clean blackboard, whereas I am full of crossed-out scribbles that I can no longer decipher.

To tell the truth, I am not sure how to manage a servant. Sometimes we are confidantes; sometimes I draw myself up and impose my authority. Maria takes advantage of my inconsistency, for I am not yet accustomed to being the mistress of a house.

I am not sure of anything. My moods, recently, have been see-sawing. Next week I have decided that Maria and I will spring-clean the house. I will engage another servant to help us. We will get down on our knees and scrub away my wicked thoughts; we will polish away the grime. Devoting myself to duty, I will punish my body until I am exhausted.

We arrive at the square. My spirits soar again. I am flooded with love for everything – the gulls, blown about in the sky like pieces of paper; the women, fondling fruit under the flapping cloths of the stalls. A dog drags itself along on its bottom; its eyes say *look at me*, as if it is performing a comic turn for my benefit. I smile at the hawkers and the quacks. '*Fresh cabbages, fresh carrots! Fresh cinnamon water! Fresh aniseed liquor, settle your stomach or your money back! Fresh plump capons, two for the price of one, hurry while stocks last!*' A boy plays colf between the women's skirts, swerving and ducking, whacking his stick against the ball.

The sun slides behind a cloud. I am suddenly overcome by repulsion. The wretched dog is not playing a joke; it has worms. Up in the belfry the bell tolls the hour for me, summoning me to atone for my sins; I am surprised nobody turns to stare. The great Weights and Measures building looms up as threatening as a tidal wave.

'Madam!' Maria nudges me. We are standing at the vegetable stall. 'I said – how many parsnips?'

The stall holder is a big, purple-faced man. He has one dead eye; it is closed in a permanent wink. I know him well, but today he seems to be leering at me as if he knows my secret. I suddenly feel naked, as peeled as the onion that will surely cause tears. These people milling around – surely they can see into my wicked heart?

Maria holds out her pail and the man tips in the parsnips. I fumble in my purse.

And then I see him. My heart jolts against my rib-cage. It is Jan van Loos, the painter. He is making his way through the crowd towards me. Today he wears a green cloak and black beret. He stops, to let a man roll a barrel past. He holds my gaze. The sounds recede like a wave retreating, hissingly, back into the ocean. For a moment I think: he just happens to be here. We will greet each other politely.

I know this isn't true. He has come here to find me; he has hunted me down. He pauses behind a poultry stall. The bald bodies dangle in front of his face, their claws clenched in a spasm of recognition. Raising his eyebrows, he indicates my maid.

I tap Maria on the shoulder. 'I'm going to the apothecary to buy some snuff.' I shove my purse into her hand. 'Finish the shopping.'

'How can you buy snuff, madam, if you have no money?'

'Ah.' I pull out some coins. My fingers feel rubbery, they won't obey me. Shoving the coins into her hand, I leave swiftly, my purse pressed to my breast as if that will protect me.

I hurry down a side-street. My path is blocked by a man pushing an ox carcass on a trolley. I press against the wall to let it pass – billowing yellow fat, the stench of it. Behind me I hear footsteps. I wait, me and my beating heart. And then he is beside me.

'I had to see you,' Jan says, catching his breath. 'All yesterday, when you were sitting there – I am quite undone.'

'Please go away.'

'You don't want me to.'

'I do! Please.'

'Say you don't want me to.' He stands there, panting. 'You want to return to that living tomb?'

'Don't you dare speak like that.'

'I can't sleep, I can't work, all I see is your sweet face –'

'Don't – please –'

'I have to know if you too are feeling –'

'I'm a married woman. I love my husband.'

The words hang in the air. We stand there breathlessly. Above us, somebody closes a window. The alley smells of drains.

Jan gazes at me and says: 'You have stolen my heart.' He takes my hand and looks at it, as if it is a thing of wonderment. He lays it against his cheek. 'I cannot live without you.' He presses my fingers to his lips.

I snatch my hand away. 'You mustn't talk to me like this. I have to go.'

'Don't go.'

I pause. 'When are you coming again to the house?'

'Next week.'

I hurry away. My skin burns; my ears are roaring.

When I reach the end of the alley I look back. With all my heart I will him to be there.

The alley is empty. Washing is strung between the houses. The bedsheets billow in the wind, as if trying to attract people's attention. *Look what's happening! Stop it before it's too late.*

✺ 10 ✺

JAN

What a loss it was for art that such a master hand
Did not use its native strength to better purpose.
Who surpassed him in the matter of painting?
But oh! The greater the talent, the more numerous the
  abberations
When it attaches itself to no principles, no rules,
But imagines it knows everything of itself.

Andries Pels on Rembrandt, 1681

Back in his studio Jan sits down heavily on a chair. He gazes at a chicken bone, lying on the floor among a scattering of walnut shells. He cannot remember when he dropped them; the bone, with its tattered flesh, is grey with dust.

Jan sits there, thinking about love. He has had many women – foolish virgins, foolish wives. For a man who devotes his life to beauty he hasn't been fussy. *There's no such thing as an ugly woman, just not enough brandy.* Of course he has loved them, after his fashion. He is a passionate man. He has whispered hot words into their ear and been sensually grateful to their bodies for responding to his. But afterwards he wishes they would go home. If they stay there, sleeping, he inches his way out of bed, pulls on his breeches and gets back to work.

It is his habit to paint at night while the city sleeps. In the silence his paintings – involuntary insomniacs –

confide in his brush as it brings them to life. To see what he is doing, however, he has to light many expensive candles and this sometimes wakes up the occupant of his bed. Just knowing that a woman is watching him, of course, breaks his concentration. Sometimes they whisper to him *come back here*. Sometimes they chastise themselves for their lapse into sin. Sometimes, worst of all, they urge him to make an honest woman of them. If only women were not so irresistible. How much simpler to suck out the flesh from an oyster and drop the shell on the floor.

Sometimes he works right through the night and falls asleep at dawn. In the morning light his painting surprises him as if it is caught unawares. How exposed it looks, with its crude colours. He has to do some repainting. If a woman stayed the night she will have left by now, in a fluster of remorse. Only his true mistress remains – badly daubed, surprised, but surrendering herself again to his brush.

Jan gets up. For once he has no appetite for work. He paces up and down and leans his head against the chimney-piece. Did Sophia Sandvoort mean it when she pushed him away? Were her protestations sincere? Maybe he has made a terrible mistake. He could not stop himself; he had to see her. It is out of his control.

The first visit it was simply lust. Sophia was a challenge but not an insurmountable one. A young woman married to a pompous old man – they were usually conquered in the end. They are a traded commodity, like a bale of flax, and though they are dutiful they don't truly love their husbands how could they? A painter seems a romantic proposition and though they fear damnation they finally surrender themselves, as long as the rules are observed.

Yesterday, however, during the second sitting, something happened. The old man was droning on . . . *tulip bulbs* . . . *de Heem* . . . How ponderously Jan's countrymen hold forth. She sat there, as modest as the Madonna in her blue dress. Suddenly they had looked at each other with such complicity. Her face spoke to him – merriment, exasperation. And something darker, something that pierced his heart.

He has astonished himself. For the first time in his dealings with women he spoke the truth. He is undone. Sophia has unknotted the ropes around his heart and he is entirely hers. He has never unclosed himself in this way before; there is a certain voluptuousness to his surrender. It is a new sensation. On the way home he passed a boy playing a penny whistle; the music filled his eyes with tears. What is he to do? Can she possibly love him?

There is a tattoo of knocks at the door. Jan freezes. It is Sophia! He breaks into a sweat. No. It is her husband. She has told him about this morning's impertinence and he has come round to kill him. He is accompanied by twelve members of the Civic Guard and they will blow his head off.

Jan opens the door. His friend Mattheus strides into the studio. 'The usual pigsty, I see,' he says cheerfully.

'Gerrit has disappeared.'

'Your servant is a drunk. You should kick him out.'

'When I can find him. The trouble is, he's never here.'

Mattheus flings himself into a chair. 'I've brought the boy.'

A youth comes in. He is pale, with long yellow hair.

'His name is Jacob.'

Jan gathers his wits. He has forgotten about this. Jacob is his new apprentice; he is due to start work today. Mattheus has arranged it because he already has three pupils of his own and no room for any more. Mattheus is a generous man – big heart, big appetites. He earns a good living painting low-life scenes: taverns and brothels. His clients find them amusing and there is usually some moral instruction somewhere, to make them feel improved. His energy is prodigious; he churns them out.

Jan searches for some glasses and wipes them on his paint rag. Mattheus unstacks canvases and leans them against the wall. He shows them to the boy.

'Look at the brushwork – look how fine it is – those clouds, that foliage. Look at the sheen on that dress, what perfection! You can almost touch it. This man can paint anything –' he chuckles '– if they pay him enough.'

'Look who's talking,' says Jan.

Mattheus gulps down some brandy and indicates Jan. 'My old friend here knows the first rule of painting.'

'What's that?' asks the boy.

'Flattery will get you everywhere –'

'Oh yes?' says Jan.

'Dress 'em up in their finery, the poor vain fools.' Mattheus points to a preliminary sketch of Sophia. 'This woman, for instance – look at that face. I'll wager you she's a dog in real life –'

'She's not!' says Jan.

'That beautiful, eh?' He snorts.

'She *is* beautiful –'

Mattheus guffaws. 'Only because you want to put your hand up her *rok*.' He turns to the boy. 'That's another technique our master here will be teaching you –'

'Curb your tongue,' says Jan. 'He's just a boy.'

Mattheus lights his pipe and blows out a cloud of smoke. 'My dearest friend, you are a highly competent painter. You'll teach this boy everything he needs to know. Except how to be truly great.' He jabs his pipe stem at Jan. 'You're so skilful, you'll get away with what you're doing all your life. You've had it too easy.' He lifts up a paintbrush. 'Know what this is?'

'It's a paintbrush,' says the boy.

'It's a paint remover.'

'Have some more brandy,' says Jan.

'Our friend Rembrandt, he understands. The more he lays on the paint, the more he strips away to reveal the truth. Do you follow me?'

The boy nods dumbly.

'The suffering, the humanity . . .' Mattheus turns to Jan. 'But you have to be courageous, my friend, and unafraid of pain. For only through pain will the beauty of the world be revealed.' He gets up and kisses Jan on both cheeks. 'I'm only saying this because I know I'll never do it myself. Underneath all this I'm a coward – just a crowd pleaser. And it's too late to change.'

Mattheus drains his glass, ruffles the boy's hair and leaves.

The boy looks at Jan. 'Aren't you angry that he talks to you like that?'

'Angry?' Jan shakes his head vigorously. 'Of course not. He talks to me like that because he loves me.'

In fact, he feels deeply uncomfortable. Hurt, too.

Feigning indifference, he spreads his legs and leans back in his chair. He looks up at the ceiling; the beams are festooned with cobwebs. Near the window he has hammered up a sagging white sheet to catch the light. Sophia is standing there, her hand on the window latch. She flings open the window and breathes deeply, inhaling the morning air. Even imagining her makes the latch dear to him. Then she turns to him, closes the window and smiles.

Jan says: 'Pass me that piece of paper, will you?'

'Are you going to give me a drawing lesson?' the boy asks.

Jan shakes his head. 'I'm going to write a note.'

❧ 11 ❧

Maria

A kitchen maid must have one eye on the pan and the other on the cat.

Johan De Brune, 1660

Maria sits beside the kitchen fire, plucking a duck. The bird is wedged between her thighs; its head hangs down as if it is inspecting the floor for crumbs. But it is dead and she suddenly wants to cry. She wants it to be alive so she can tell it her secrets. This is ridiculous. She must have plucked hundreds of ducks. Back in the country, where she grew up, she cheerfully wrung their necks too. Lately, however, she has been overcome with pity for those that suffer, even dumb creatures. It is like her love for Willem – 'Willem . . . Willem . . .' she whispers his name. She feels peeled and whimpery. *If you peel an onion you'll cry*, said her grandmother. Now she knows what she was talking about.

Her granny was full of wise sayings. Maria remembers her churning butter. Sleeves rolled up, she leant over the barrel vigorously pumping the pole, twisting it this way and that. *Only from commotion comes the fat*, she said. *Hard work will be rewarded.* When Maria grew older her grandmother said that the cream was the spirit and the whey was fleshly pleasure. Maria didn't understand her, then.

The cat watches the duck. Its tail twitches. Maria is

superstitious. If the cat scratches itself, Willem will knock at the door. The cat has fleas; it won't be long now.

There is a knock at the door. Maria jumps up, dumps the duck on the table and hurries out.

She unlatches the door. A youth stands there. He hands her an envelope. 'Please give this to the mistress of the house,' he says.

Maria, disappointed, takes the letter and closes the door. She walks upstairs to the bedchamber. Since their shopping trip this morning her mistress has been feeling unwell and has shut herself in her room.

Downstairs in the kitchen the cat jumps on to the table. It sinks its claws into the duck's flesh.

❧ 12 ❧

THE LETTER

Thy wife shall be as a fruitful vine upon the walls of thy house; thy children like the olive branches around thy table. Lo, thus shall man be blessed that feareth the Lord.

Psalm 128

Sophia stands at the window. She is reading the letter. Through the glass, sunlight streams on to her face. Her hair is pulled back from her brow. Tiny pearls nestle in her headband; they catch the light, winking at the severity of her coiffure. She wears a black bodice, shot with lines of velvet and silver. Her dress is violet silk; its pewtery sheen catches the light.

Behind her a tapestry is strung along a wooden rail. Paintings can be glimpsed in the shadows. The green velvet curtains around the bed are pulled back to reveal an opulent bedcover. The room is bathed in tranquil golden light.

She stands there, motionless. She is suspended, caught between past and present. She is colour, waiting to be mixed; a painting, ready to be brushed into life. She is a moment, waiting to be fixed for ever under a shiny varnish. Is this a moment of decision? Will she tear up the letter or will she steal away, through the silent rooms, and slip out of the house? Her face, caught in profile, betrays nothing.

Outside, the street is busy. Two regents, sitting in a

46

carriage, rattle over the bridge. They nod to each other; what they say is of importance to them. A barrel is winched down from a warehouse door, high in a building, and rolled on to a barge; when painted into the background, its contents will for ever be unknown. A group of Mennonite men huddle like crows on the corner; children brush past them, yelling.

Outside all is bustle. Indoors a heart stands still.

The letter says: *It is too late. We both know that. I must see you, my love. Come to my studio tomorrow at four.*

～§ 13 §～

JAN

If you would have me weep, you must first of all feel grief yourself.

Horace, *Ars Poetica*

The sandglass has emptied. Jan turns it upside down for the second time. It is five o'clock. She is not going to come.

How foolish, to think she would. Gerrit has swept the floor and tidied up the room. This morning his servant returned, chastened and purple-faced, from his drinking binge, but Jan was too distracted to be angry with him. Remorse always makes Gerrit punctilious; he has even rubbed clean the window-panes, after his fashion. The table is laid for two: smoked meat, cheese, wine and marzipan tarts, powdered with sugar, that Jan bought this morning. Gerrit has been banished to the kitchen. The boy has been sent home.

Sophia will not come. How mad he is to imagine, for a moment, that she might. Why should she risk everything for him? He can offer her nothing, only love.

The sand, just a thread, falls through the pinched waist of the hourglass. So far just a pimple rests on the bottom. As Jan watches, it grows. He doesn't even know Sophia. He feels he has known her all his life, she has made her home in his heart, but he is just a deluded fool. For a fleeting moment he is actually glad that she's not

48

coming, for if she stays away she will be saved from possible ruination. He is actually worried for *her*. This is not like him. But then none of this is.

The heap of sand increases. The bigger it grows, the more his hopes fade. Outside in the street two men bellow drunkenly. Jan's neighbourhood, Jordaan, is too disreputable for a refined lady like Sophia. He looks around the studio and sees it through her eyes. The white sheet pinned saggingly to the ceiling; its accompanying cobwebs. The plinth, draped with cloth, where his models sit. On the walls hang curling prints; a large crack runs from floor to ceiling. Plaster casts – a hand, a leg – dangle from hooks. The whole place reeks of linseed oil.

Jan comes from a family of craftsmen. His father is a silversmith and his two brothers are glass painters. He is used to living among the tools of his trade, but how could he have expected a gentlewoman like Sophia to gamble on her reputation for this? He has even had clean sheets put on his bed, in idiotic readiness.

The sandglass is half filled. She is not coming. Jan sits down on the chest and pulls on his shoes. He gazes for the last time at the meal – the long-stemmed wine-glasses, the bowl of fruit, the powdered tartlets. Like a still life they will sit there, stilled at four o'clock, for ever unconsumed. They are objects pregnant with possibilities, with a future that will now only exist in his imagination. He looks at them with an artist's eye: the white cloth distorted through the twin glasses, the metallic gleam of knife and jug. Despite everything, this harmonious arrangement pleasures his senses.

'Gerrit!' he calls. 'Clear the table. I'm going to the tavern.'

He hears a faint sound. At first he thinks it is the tree outside, tapping at the window. He gets up and puts on his cloak. His legs feel leaden, as if he has been wading through a bog.

He hears the tapping again. It is at the door.

Jan strides across and opens it.

Sophia stands there. 'It's me,' she says.

⇜§ 14 §⇝

MARIA

Love can neither be bought nor sold – its only price is love.
Jacob Cats, *Moral Emblems*, 1632

Maria sits side by side with Willem on the back step. The sun is sinking; the high wall casts the courtyard into shadow. It is a small, enclosed yard and receives the sun only briefly at this time of year. Her broom leans against the wall like a sentry.

Willem strokes her fingers one by one. 'You should rub some fat into these, my lovely. Goosefat. That'll make you a lady.'

'It'll take more than that,' Maria laughs.

She leans against him. The stone step freezes her bottom but she doesn't dare move with him into the house; she is not sure if her mistress is still at home. The letter seemed to have upset her; maybe it contained bad news from her family. Since yesterday her mistress has been acting strangely. Twice this afternoon she put on her cloak to go out and then took it off again. The last time Maria saw her she was sitting next to the front door twisting a tendril of her hair around her finger.

'Maria, my darling, I've got something to ask you.'

'What is it?'

'I love you and you love me.' Willem puts his hand around her waist. 'I think I'm right in saying that.'

'Of course I love you. Yesterday I blubbed over a duck.

I feel all shivery when I see you. Can't you tell?'

'So you and me – let's get married.'

She nods. Happiness floods her. Over the wall, in the apple tree next door, a blackbird pours out its song like coins, like sweet wine, oh her head is spinning.

'Of course I want to marry you, Willem, but we don't have any money.'

'You wait.' He taps the side of his nose. 'I've got plans.'

'What plans?'

'I can't divulge them, not at this moment. Suffice it to say that I'm going to make a lady of you and we'll have a place to live and then we can have babies.'

Babies. Maria closes her eyes. There are six of them, always six. She can feel them already, fighting for a place on her knee. In her dreams they are fishes but now they are suddenly, sturdily, real. Their laughter echoes with the bird-song.

'How are you going to find this money?' Maria asks.

Willem takes her hand and presses it to his heart. 'Trust me, oh my sweetness, my love.' Already, like a husband, he is taking control. Even his voice sounds deeper. 'Let's just call it a business venture.'

He wants to marry her! Maria gazes at the single flowerbed. Shoots have pushed through the soil; how hopeful they are. Lumps of earth have been dislodged by their blunt, blind determination. Spring is here at last. She leans her head on Willem's shoulder and thinks: in all this city there are no two people as happy as us.

❦ 15 ❧

SOPHIA

Those who wade in unknown waters will be sure to be drowned.

Jacob Cats, *Moral Emblems*, 1632

Jan lives on the ground floor of a house in the Bloem-gracht, but a mile from my home. He wants to escort me part of the way back, but we must not be seen together so I slip out of his studio and hurry down the street. The sun is sinking; the sky blushes pink for me. The whole city is blushing, her buildings ruddy with shock. The canal is molten. The water, reflected on the houses, dances on the brickwork. The windows are on fire.

Between my legs I am damp from love. *Only an hour – I can only stay an hour.* What an hour that was. If I have no other, I shall remember it all my life.

I cross the Wester-Markt, my head down, and cut through a side-street. I hurry like a criminal escaping from the scene of my wickedness. The lower parts of the houses here are whitewashed – paint roughly splashed around their doors and windows. If only I, in such a way, could conceal my blemishes.

'Sophia my dear! Fancy seeing you here.'

I stagger back; we nearly collided.

'Are you walking this way? What a charming dress, you must tell me where you purchased the material.'

It is Mrs Mijtins, our lawyer's wife. She hurries along beside me.

'You must tell me your secret.'

'What do you mean?' I ask sharply.

'You've been keeping it so well hidden. You promised to tell me but you never did.'

'Tell you what?'

'The name of your dressmaker, of course. Remember, when you came to our musical evening? Mine is utterly incompetent, she came recommended by Mrs Overvalt but she hardly knows how to turn a hem. And the wretched girl always seems to have a running cold. My, you *do* look well! Burgundy suits you – *such* a pretty fabric – it brings out the colour in your cheeks. If only my daughters had your looks – slow down, dear. Oh those young legs! I can hardly keep up with you.'

ஜ 16 ஜ

JAN

The draperies that clothe figures must show that they are inhabited by these figures, enveloping them neatly to show the posture and motion of such figures, and avoiding the confusion of many folds, especially over the prominent parts, so that these may be evident.

Leonardo da Vinci, *Notebooks*

Painting is an act of possession. All objects, however humble, are gazed upon with the same focused sensuality. Animal, vegetable or mineral, they are all equal; the curve of an earthenware jug is as lovingly painted as a woman's breast. An artist's passion is truly dispassionate.

Now, however, it is different, for he has possessed her. This is the third and final sitting; after today he will take the canvas home and complete it in his studio. Now Jan has touched the body beneath the dress, now he has held Sophia naked in his arms, he is paralysed. This demure, seated wife is his sweetheart. She is no longer an arrangement of cobalt-blue dress, fur-trimmed jacket and pale skin tones. His composition has been disordered by love.

Sophia is radiant; she blazes. Surely her husband can sense it, next to him? Cornelis may be a pedantic old fool but how could he not feel the charge in the room?

These questions are distracting. Jan realizes that he has been standing, brush in hand, for minutes on end.

Cornelis must notice. The apparitions on Jan's canvas, gaining ghostly shape – these figments of his imagination that bear a passing resemblance to real people – they look rebuffed, as if he has betrayed them too. His brush strokes Sophia into being, but in the painting she will be locked for ever into wifeliness, a woman sitting obediently beside her husband.

That is his excuse, that he has lost her. Jan fears, however, that he cannot paint the truth of her; it is beyond his powers. He blames the convention in which he is trapped, but if he were a great painter she would come alive and radiate love to everyone who will gaze at her on the canvas. They will understand that she is capable of passion. He must convey that or he has failed.

As he paints he hears her voice. *I loved you from the first moment I saw you.*

How surprising she was! He thought that she would swoon from guilt and remorse.

It's too late for that now. I wanted to come. I want to be here. Nothing matters, only this.

When they climbed into his bed he was so overcome that at first he had failed her. *What – I've ruined myself for nothing?* she had whispered, laughing.

I can't believe that you're here, he had replied.

She had taken his hand. *I'm just a woman – here, feel . . . just flesh and blood.*

The world is chaotic. All artists know this, but they try to make sense of it. Sophia has made sense of it for him. She has stitched it together like the most beautiful cloak. Her love has sewn it together and they can wrap it around themselves and be safe from the world. Nobody can reach them.

Except that they have had one hour alone together and this is her life and Cornelis is here and why cannot he die?

The library floor is laid with black and white marble squares. It is a human chessboard. Jan narrows his eyes until the room blurs. He lifts up his queen, Sophia. He lands her on the other side of her husband. Then he picks up the husband and flings him away.

Jan packs up. Cornelis bids him goodbye and goes into another room. They hear his footsteps recede; a far door closes.

Sophia accompanies Jan to the door. 'I was nearly discovered,' she whispers. 'A woman saw me, a woman I know.'

They swing round.

Maria, tears streaming down her face, comes running across the room. She holds a bird by its leg. 'The cat killed it. Look – it's the blackbird that sings in the apple tree next door.'

'Poor thing.' Sophia looks at it. 'But don't cry.'

'It meant so much to me,' sobs Maria. 'And you know what's going to happen when a blackbird dies –'

'Maria! Stop it.' Sophia ushers Jan into the street.

'Eleven o'clock tomorrow morning,' whispers Jan. He drops his paint rag. Sophia bends down to pick it up with him. 'At the footbridge . . .' He whispers the name of the street.

'I'm going to bury it in the flowerbed,' says the maid.

❧ 17 ❧

SOPHIA

The praise of a woman mainly exists in the care she gives to her household. For the turtle is always at home, and carries its house along under all circumstance.

J. van Beverwijck, 1639

It is raining. I hurry down the Street of Cheeses, down towards the harbour. The place is deserted. In the shops the huge Goudas sit like boulders; they sit in judgement.

Maybe he won't come – not now it is raining. Maybe he doesn't love me enough. I wish there were some people around. There is safety in crowds; I feel exposed, hurrying along alone. Yet my heart pounds with excitement.

Over the past week the city has been transformed. Even if he does not come today he exists, he breathes this air and walks these streets. Every building is dear to me because it is also familiar to him. Yet it is a city of the utmost danger. The houses stand here, slap up against the street; they gaze into it. So many windows, the houses are crammed with windows – vast windows here at street level, closest to me, windows jammed together on the upper floors, rows of spying windows topped by a spy-hole up at the top, in the gables. Some shutters are closed; some half open. Shadows lurk behind the latticed glass. Behind an open casement – why is it open? – a curtain stirs.

And then there are all those corners. They are laid with gunpowder, danger waits around each of them. *Sophia! Fancy seeing you here.* How easily I can be betrayed by those who mean me no harm.

I slip round a corner. The wind slaps my face. I lean into it but it tries to blow me back, back to the Herengracht where I belong. It is March, but winter has returned; my face is numb with cold. I hurry along beside the canal; the salt air stings my nostrils. The merchants' houses are tall here, six stories high. Up above me doors open into space. Hoists jut from them; hooks hang suspended above my head.

Then I see him. Ahead of me is the footbridge; Jan is hurrying towards me on the other side of the canal. He waves; my heart lurches. I knew he would come. I quicken my steps. A boat is approaching. In a few minutes the footbridge will break open, separating me from my beloved. Laughing, I race towards it.

Jan stops. For a split second I wonder why. Then I see three men, dressed in black, emerging from a warehouse. One of them is my husband. He breaks away from the group and approaches me.

'My dear love, what are you doing here? You're soaked.'

My mind works quickly. Down a side-street I see a surgeon's pole, jutting from a shop. It is striped red, white and blue – red for bleeding, blue for a shave and white for fractures and teeth pulling.

'I have to have a tooth pulled,' I say. 'I have a terrible toothache.'

'But why didn't you tell me? Why don't you go to the surgeon in the Prinsengracht?'

'Mrs Mijtins recommended this one.'

'I will accompany you.' Cornelis turns to the men. 'Be so kind and wait for me back in the office.'

'No, go back to your work.'

'But –'

'Please, sir. I will be all right. And look – the rain has stopped.'

'But you cannot return unaccompanied, you'll be feeling unwell –'

'Maria is coming to collect me. Please go.'

Cornelis pauses, stroking his beard. The two men wait restlessly. I know I have won.

He kisses me on the cheek and then he leaves. I walk down the side-street towards the surgeon's shop. Behind me I hear footsteps.

It is Jan. He cups my elbow and steers me into a tavern. We sit down at a table. The place is half empty; I recognize nobody here. Besides, I am not a frequenter of alehouses and this one is some distance from my home.

'What are we going to do?' I ask him. 'If I go to your studio I'll be seen. Sooner or later I'll be seen.'

'You look so beautiful.' Gazing at me, Jan rubs my face with his handkerchief. 'Come home to my bed.'

'I cannot! I'll be seen.'

'Come when it's dark.'

'I will still be seen.'

'My darling, I cannot live without you.'

A girl brings us glasses of beer. On the wall hangs a birdcage. Inside it a parrot moves along its perch, claw by claw. It moves as close to us as it can get; then it cocks its head and watches us with one eye.

'And now I'm believed to have a tooth missing,' I say.

'I would pull all my teeth out for you.'

'No! I've got one old man already, isn't that enough?'

Suddenly we burst into laughter. We lean against each other, shaking. How can I mock my husband? I will be consumed by the fires of hell.

'How can you bear him to kiss you?'

'Don't –'

'Those scrawny arms around you, *I* cannot bear it –'

'Stop it!'

It is true, of course. Cornelis's sour breath . . . his grey, loose skin . . . the other part I cannot bear to think about – but I keep quiet. Isn't this treachery enough?

Under the table Jan takes my hand. 'Come to me tonight.'

I gaze at him – his wild wet hair, his blue eyes. And I am lost.

'Why are you not ready?' asks Cornelis. 'It is six o'clock.'

'I don't want to go.'

'But you enjoy playing cards with the Konicks. Last time you won, remember? And they have just taken delivery of a spinet. You told them last week how much you wanted to try it.'

'My tooth still hurts.'

'Oh my poor dear – let me look –'

I move back. 'No –'

'It must be painful –'

'The oil of camphor eases the pain but I want to have an early night.'

'Then I will stay with you.'

'No!'

'It is no pleasure without you by my side.'

'I would rather be alone,' I reply. 'I am no company tonight. Truly, dearest – I will go to bed early. Please go – they are your oldest friends – please, I beg you.'

Cornelis fetches his cloak and goes to the door. Suddenly I run after him and fling my arms around his neck. Surprised, he turns; our noses bump. This awkwardness throws us off balance.

'I'm so sorry,' I mutter into his beard.

'Sorry? To show me such affection?' He holds me tightly.

Just for a moment I wish none of this had happened. If only we could turn back the clock and be as we were – contented, safe within these rooms. I cannot recognize this new woman whose heart beats within me – an impostor, who should be thrown out of this house in disgrace.

'I am unworthy of you,' I whisper.

'How can you say that?' He smooths my hair. 'You are my joy, my life.'

We embrace, again, and then he is gone.

❧ 18 ❧

WILLEM

Every man is the architect of his own fortune.
Jacob Cats, *Moral Emblems*, 1632

Dusk is falling. Willem makes his way towards the Herengracht. The wind has died down. It has been a wild day with a gale blowing from the Baltic. No fishing boats could put to sea. Another whale has been washed up a few miles along the coast. Unlike Maria, he knows that this is a good omen. He has made his living from fish and look! Today of all days the ocean has belched up the most magnificent catch. God is on his side.

Willem walks briskly, a spring to his step. Countless times, bowed by his basket, he has plodded these streets. This evening the only weight he feels is the purse in his jerkin. He cannot wait to see Maria's face. She didn't believe him when they sat in the garden. *Let's just call it a business venture.*

He is still numb with shock. Normally he is not a gambling man but these are not normal times. Before today, before everything changed, he had considered them *kappisten* – hooded ones, madmen. But he has joined the tulip speculators now and who is he to consider it lunacy?

Money can multiply, just like that. How truly miraculous! . . . A few meetings, his new friends huddled in a cloud of tobacco smoke; numbers, senseless to him,

chalked on a board. Packages passed from hand to hand
... How astoundingly easy it has been, for he has
gambled at random and struck lucky each time. Until
recently money has been doggedly earned – a florin here,
some stuivers there, a handful of coins. He has worked
himself to exhaustion, rising at dawn to tramp down to
the fish market, hail and sleet, all weathers. He never
complained because he is not that sort, but truly he was
a *kappisten* then. Icy fish, icy fingers pulling out slobbery
strings of guts. Bent with his basket, he has tramped the
streets in blistering wind, knocking on doors and trying
to smile though his face is frozen. Only the thought of
Maria has kept him warm.

Maria! Forget whales; she is his prize catch. She says
she loves him and he still cannot believe it. He has had
little experience of women. They don't take him
seriously. It is something about his face; it makes them
giggle. They have been affectionate enough but when
he has tried to make love to them they have burst into
laughter. They call him 'clown-face' and when he looks
doleful they laugh louder, saying he looks even funnier.
It hurts his feelings.

Now he has Maria. But has he? Can she really love
him? She is so pretty – plump and ripe like a fruit. And
she is such a flirt. *The vegetable man was showing me his
carrots.* Men look at her in the street; she challenges
them with her bold stare. Can he trust her? *Of course I love
you. I go all shivery when I see you.* She refuses to marry him
until he has some money. That is understandable; she is
a practical woman. Well, wait until he opens his purse;
see her face then.

Maria is not expecting him; he will surprise her.

Tonight her master and mistress have gone out to play cards; she will be alone. Even so, Willem approaches the side door, down the alleyway, the one he uses when he steals in after dark.

Willem stops dead. A figure emerges from the door. She closes it behind her and hurries off, away down the alley. It is Maria. She slips like a shadow between the buildings.

Willem is going to call out but something stops him. Maria looks so purposeful, so intent. He follows her down the alley, keeping his distance. There is something odd about her. She emerges into the Keisergracht and glances to the right and the left. He can glimpse her more clearly now. Under her shawl she wears her white cap, the one with long flaps that conceal her face.

She turns right and hurries along, keeping close to the houses. How furtive she looks! She moves fast; he has to break into a trot to keep her in sight. This, too, is unlike Maria. She usually ambles, swaying her hips, taking her time.

For a moment he loses her. She has darted left, down the Berenstraat. A dog barks, flinging itself against a closed door. Where is she going, and why so fast? It is dark now. She avoids the main thoroughfares; she darts down side alleys, flitting like a ghost. Behind shutters, men roar with laughter. Light briefly illuminates her, as she passes a window. Then she is gone, swallowed up by the night.

She is running now. How light she is, she is almost flying! Willem pants behind her, keeping his distance. But she never turns, she seems oblivious. Pots clatter in kitchens; roasting meat mingles with the smell of drains.

Behind doors people are eating their dinners but Willem feels oddly sealed off. It is as if he and this flitting figure have become detached from the normal life of the city. It is just him and her, drawn by some powerful tide. His lungs burn; his purse bumps against his thigh.

They are in the Bloemgracht now. Maria taps at a door. Willem hides behind one of the trees that line the street. He hears a tiny, wet sneeze, strangely human. It is a puppy, playing in the dust. It darts at his leg; he nudges it away with his foot.

The door opens. Candle-light flickers on Maria, briefly, and she steps in.

Willem's heart is hammering. He crosses the street and approaches the window. The lower half is closed by shutters. The upper glass, however, is illuminated from within. Willem thinks: perhaps it is a doctor's house. Somebody is ill and Maria has run here for help. He thinks: maybe she is friends with a servant here, to whom she has lent some household item. She needs to retrieve it before her master and mistress return.

Why then is his heart beating so fast? There is a bench beside the front door. Willem climbs on to it.

He looks down, into the room. He sees bare floorboards, an easel and a chair. For a moment he thinks that the room is empty but he hears faint voices. Then they move into view.

It is Maria and a man. He cannot see Maria's face; she is below him, her back to the window. The man is laughing. He rests his forehead against hers, shaking with laughter. His black curly hair presses against her cap.

Then she takes his head in her hands. It is a gesture of

the utmost tenderness. She raises his face to hers, her hands threaded through his hair. She holds his face in her hands as if it is the most precious object she has ever held. And then she kisses him.

Willem's legs buckle beneath him. He slides down to a sitting position. Then he gets up and stumbles away, blindly.

❧ 19 ☙

SOPHIA

Fresh mussels can be compared to
The blessed women-folk
Who speak modestly and virtuously
And always look after their household;
All wives must regularly bear
The burden of their mussel-house.

Adriaen van de Venne, *Tableau of Foolish senses*, 1623

Jan has already turned the sandglass upside down again. Time is running out, for when this hour has trickled through I must go. How strange, that a heap of sand has contained so much joy! Jan's past is in there too, measured in grains, but these two hours belong to us.

'If you were a truly great painter –'

'If?' he snorts. '*If?*'

'Could you paint an hourglass and fill the painting with such joy that everyone who sees it can understand what has happened?'

He gazes at me tenderly. 'Has it ever happened to anyone else like this?'

We are lying on his bed. Jan drinks from his glass. Then he turns my face to his, opens my lips and spills the sweet wine into my mouth. 'It's you I want to paint – now – just as you are.'

'No, don't leave me.'

He strokes my cheek with his thumb. 'How could I possibly?'

Maria's clothes, my spent disguise, lie on the floor. They look somehow emptier than normal clothes, as if exhausted by the role they have had to play. They are my chrysalis; I split them and emerged, a creature transformed. I am a butterfly whose life span is just one hour.

Jan slices a piece of ham. I watch the muscles of his back shift under his skin. 'You like the fat?'

I nod greedily. He slides the slice of ham into my mouth. It is the most corrupt of sacraments. Ah but it is delicious!

'I'm committing a mortal sin,' I say, my mouth full. 'Has God put His hands over His face and turned the other way?'

Jan shakes his head. 'God's watching us. If He truly loves us, if He's a generous God, won't He want us to be happy?'

I swallow the ham. 'Your faith is like putty. How easily you mould it to your own desires.'

He spills more wine into my mouth. 'Drink His blood then, see if it makes you feel better.'

'That's wicked!' I splutter.

Suddenly the mood is broken. 'You know what's wicked? You know what's a sin?' Jan's voice rises. 'That you're locked up in that great tomb with somebody you don't love –'

'No –'

'Who's caged you up, who's sucking the life out of you to warm his old bones –'

'That's not true!'

'Who's bought you like one of his precious paintings and you've let yourself be bought!'

'I've not! You don't know anything. He's a kind man. You mustn't talk about him like this. He supports my mother and my sisters, he's saved my family, without him they'd be destitute –'

'Exactly. He's bought you.'

I start crying. Jan holds me in his arms. He kisses my wet face – my nose, my eyes. I sob because I cannot bear him to tell me this and now our moment is ruined. And all the time the sand is running out.

'Forgive me, my love,' he murmurs. 'I'm just jealous.'

'Of *him*?'

'Of what he has – your sweet face, your sweetness in his house . . .' He stops.

I cannot tell him the truth, not yet. How the thought of going back to my husband's bed repulses me. I still feel loyalty to Cornelis, even while I am betraying him.

I say: 'I am not really in the house. I don't exist there. I'm like an empty husk, like those clothes. I have disappeared from there.' This seems just as much a betrayal, but now I've said it and it is too late.

Jan gazes at me. I point to the print hanging on the wall next to the dismembered plaster limbs. It's a *Day of Judgement*. God, in a shaft of light, sits above the writhing bodies. 'Can you turn that the other way?' I whisper.

Jan jumps up and tears the print off the wall. It falls to the floor. Then he comes to me one last time before the sand runs out.

WILLEM

Where the wine is in, the wit is out.

Jacob Cats, *Moral Emblems*, 1632

Willem staggers through the streets. He is sobbing; his heart is broken. It is pitch dark; the light in his life has been extinguished. He has walked a long way; he is somewhere near the Nieuwendijk. He feels the chillness of water beside him. Why not just fling himself into the canal and end this torment?

He hears a roar of laughter. Ahead, he sees a tavern. Light glows through its windows. He hears music and voices raised in song. He hesitates. Where else can he go? What else is he to do now his life is in ruins?

He pushes open the door. A smell of sweat and tobacco fills his nostrils. The room is crammed with people; how oblivious they are in their merriment! A fiddler scrapes his violin. Women sit on men's knees, weighing them down; they shift their buttocks, making themselves at home. Couples are dancing, bumping into the furniture. Customers bang their mugs on the table, singing lustily.

> 'On Monday morning I married a wife
> Thinking to live a sober life
> But as it turned out I'd better been dead
> Than rue the day that I got wed!'

Serving girls, holding foaming pitchers of beer, push their way between the bodies. Choking in the tobacco smoke, Willem sits down.

> 'On Tuesday morning I went to the wood
> Thinking to do my wife some good,
> I cut a twig of holly so green,
> The roughest and toughest that ever was seen . . .'

'What's up with you, you miserable *gek*? Come to drown your sorrows?'

The man sitting next to him raises his eyebrows. Willem wipes his nose on his sleeve. Blubbing, at his age! The humiliation of it.

'Women,' Willem replies. 'Women trouble.' He speaks like a man of experience.

The fellow nods his head. 'Women! They're all the same. Can't trust 'em an inch, the *sletten*.'

> 'I walloped her leg and I walloped her wig,
> Until I broke my holly twig . . .'

He has a kind face, this fellow. His cheek is disfigured by a scar. It runs to his chin, pulling down one eye. This gives him a sorrowful look. He too has been in the wars.

> 'On Sunday morning I dined without
> A scolding wife or a bawling bout,
> I could enjoy my bottle and friend
> And have a fresh wife at the week's work's end!'

Willem decides to confide in his fellow drinker. He tells

him how much he loved Maria and the surprise he was bringing her tonight.

'I'm not a gambling man, you understand, but I thought I would give it a try. This fellow I know, he tipped me the wink. Admiral Pottebackers, they're the ones, he said, they're going to go through the roof. A small investment now and in a couple of months you'll rake it in. I liked the name, being a patriotic sort of fellow, and seeing the ships go by where I grew up. There was other admirals to choose from, plenty of tulips called admirals' names, but I plumped for that.'

'And did you?'

'What?' asks Willem.

'Rake it in?'

Willem nods and pats his purse. 'Know what I started with, what I scraped together? Nearly ruined me, too. Ten florins.'

'And how much is in there?'

Tears well into Willem's eyes. 'I was going to tell her tonight – I can put this money towards a little shop, maybe with lodgings above, I won't have to tramp the streets, I can give her a home and we can get married.' He starts sobbing.

'How much, you poor tosspot?'

'Seventy-eight florins, that's how much.' Willem wipes his nose on his sleeve. 'It's a blessed miracle. I don't make that much money in six months, not unless I'm lucky, it's a miracle come to me just like that, just a few old bulbs, but where's my darling to share it?'

The fellow seems to have bought him a brandy. Willem gulps it down; it burns his throat.

'Women!' says the man. 'Fuck 'em.' He snorts with

laughter. 'Fuck 'em, that's all they're good for.'

He clicks his fingers; Willem's glass is refilled.

'Drink up, we've all been diddled by them, the scheming little cows, but you're with friends here. And this is an honest place – can't be too careful, carrying cash like that around – it's an honest establishment, they don't water the wine here, they don't stuff rags in the beer pitchers, not like some places I know.'

> 'A boy to me was bound apprentice
> Because his parents they were poor
> I took him from the Haarlem poorhouse
> All for to sail on the Spanish shore . . .'

Willem's head swims; he is unaccustomed to strong spirits. Then there is a girl sitting opposite him. She seems to have appeared from nowhere.

'Allow me to introduce my little sister Annetje,' says the man. 'She's had her heart broken too, haven't you, my sweet?'

The girl sighs. 'Oh, I've been led up the garden path and no mistake.'

'My poor little innocent sis,' says the fellow. 'This is –'

'Willem.'

'That's a nice name.' She is not as pretty as Maria; she has a bony little face with two pink blotches on her cheeks. But when she smiles her eyes twinkle. 'Where do you come from, Willem?'

He tells her the name of his fishing village. 'It's just a little place, you won't know of it.'

'Oh yes, I do,' she replies. 'I was born near there.' She moves round and sits next to him, nice and snug. 'You and me, we're two of a kind.' She gestures around the room. 'They don't understand what it's like for us, this big wicked city, what it's like for you and me. This man, he lured me here. He said he loved me and then when I wouldn't submit to his filthy lust – I'm only a poor girl but I'm keeping my precious gift, it's the only treasure I possess – when I wouldn't submit to him he threw me out, into the street, without even a goodbye.' Her eyes are brimming with tears. 'I loved him just like you did, like you said.'

Willem puts his arm around her. He can feel her sharp shoulders; compared with his comfortable Maria she feels as frail as a bird. 'Don't cry,' he says. 'I'll look after you.'

More drinks are put in front of them. Annetje raises her glass. 'Here's to us and the folks back home.'

He gulps it down. Warmth spreads through him; the room sways. 'She's so pretty,' he says. 'I knew she couldn't love a dolt like me.'

Annetje snuggles against him. 'I think she's stupid. *I* think you're very handsome.' She puts her hand on his knee.

He is on a ship; the room rocks to and fro. Bunches of hops, hanging from the ceiling, sway in time to the stamping feet. Annetje's brother seems to have disappeared.

'Here's a health to the man and the maid,
Here's a health to the jolly dragoon,
We've tarried here all day and drunk down the sun
Let's tarry here and drink down the moon!'

He gazes around. He loves them all. Dimmed by smoke, they seem to be dancing in a dream and now Annetje has dragged him to his feet and they are dancing too, except his feet won't do what he tells them to do. He staggers; she props him upright. She grips him tight; she has strong little arms. Up on the wall a row of plates loom forward and recede, surely they will topple down and crash?

Time passes; he seems to have been here for ever. The music quickens and now Annetje is laughing. Her teeth are stained by tobacco; with a vague sort of surprise he realizes that she is very young, hardly more than a girl. Where is her brother? The fellow should be looking after her. She presses herself against Willem and he feels a shameful stir of desire. How could he, when he loves Maria? *The minx. The trollop. Fuck 'em.*

'You're happy now.' Annetje giggles in his ear. 'Something tells me you're getting *very* happy.' She clutches him tighter, rubbing herself against him. 'Want to take me home?'

He nods. He must look after her. She is lost, like himself; they must comfort each other. And her hard, insistent little body is making his bones melt.

She leads him through the crowd. An old lady grins at them, baring her gums. She says something to Annetje, who leans over and whispers in her ear. Somebody bumps against Willem; he staggers and regains his balance. Looking at the woman again, he realizes that she is not old, in fact – hardly beyond thirty years. His brain is befuddled. Nothing, tonight, is what it seems.

Gripping his hand, Annetje leads him upstairs.

'Where do you live?' he asks.

'My lodgings is here,' she says. 'I've got a little room.

We're one big happy family.'

They walk down a narrow passage. There are doors both sides. Behind one of them a woman shrieks with laughter. It's an eerie sound, like a bird he used to hear at night on the marshes.

And then Annetje has closed the door behind them. It is a tiny room, just space for a bed. Willem's wits are slow at the best of times; it is only now that, drunkenly, he realizes what she is. For a moment he is disappointed; another dream vanishes. Then he is relieved. She is a prostitute. He doesn't have to protect her now, he can do what he wants with her.

The thought arouses him. He has never been with a prostitute before but all the other fellows have – the fishermen he deals with, the stall holders down in the market. Even his younger brother Dierk, if he can believe him.

'Don't be shy,' Annetje whispers, pulling him on to the bed. She lies next to him. It is a tight fit; he is jammed against the wall. She takes his hand under her skirt and pushes his finger into her hole. How warm and slippery it is! 'See how wet you've made me?' she groans. 'Something tells me you're a big boy . . . Got a surprise for me in there?'

With fast, expert fingers she unlaces Willem's breeches and slides her hand inside. His member is standing up stiff and strong. 'Fuck me!' she gasps. Her surprise sounds genuine. His member is indeed enormous. When he was younger it had embarrassed him, this great heavy thing rearing up, but now he feels a certain innocent pride in it. 'Funny puppy's face,' she says. 'You'd never guess it . . . what a truncheon!'

She strokes it; her breath quickens. He too can hardly bear it. He is trembling; in a moment he will spurt through her fingers.

'Aren't I the lucky girl tonight,' she murmurs.

'How much?' This is what a man should ask.

'A joy-stick like yours, I'll do you for free.'

She lays him on his back, hoists up her skirts and starts to mount him. Then she pauses. 'Oh-oh, nature calls,' she says. 'Must have a piss, be back in a moment.' She climbs off him, bends down and gives it a kiss. 'Now you stay there, you big bad boy.'

The door closes. Her footsteps patter away down the passage.

Willem lies there, throbbing. His confused brain can hardly remember what has happened tonight. Maria? She is lost to him now. The bed gently rocks on the swell of his inebriation. He feels seasick, but not unpleasantly so. He has joined the men now; soon he will be inside her hot little *kut* and he can do what he likes with her, nothing will surprise her. He gazes down his body. Sturdily, in eager anticipation, the crimson head rears up.

I'll do you for free. His heart swells. If Maria could see him now! A tough little whore and she's going to do him for nothing. That's the sort of man Maria has spurned. He lies there, grinning. *Aren't I the lucky girl tonight*!

Maybe he should give her a tip, to show his appreciation. He rummages in his jerkin.

Later he remembers this moment. The rhythmic thumps against the wall, the muffled giggles. The ceiling beam that smites his head when he jumps up.

Willem is downstairs, back in the tavern. Laughter roars;

the violin scrapes gratingly. Reddened faces leer at him as he pushes through the crowd.

He grabs the tavern keeper. 'Where's she gone?' he yells.

'Who're you talking about?'

'That *zakkeroller*! She's stolen my purse!'

'Never seen her.' The man pulls away. 'Excuse me.'

'Where's her brother?'

'Who?'

He isn't her brother, of course. 'They've stolen my money!' he screams.

'Who're you accusing?'

A fist punches Willem's chin, pushing his head into his chest. The room reels. Somebody seems to be laughing – how could they laugh? Willem falls awkwardly to the floor, pulling a chair with him. Feet kick him and now he feels himself being dragged out of the door, his back bumping over the steps, dragged out into the cold street. He's yanked to his feet.

'Get out of here, you scum!'

Somebody hits him again, hard across the face. He buckles with the pain; his nose is bursting. He tries to shield his face but his arms are wrenched back.

And then he's being pushed away. He stumbles against the low wall of the canal. Somebody lifts his leg up. Willem tries to kick him off but there are several men now, pushing him.

He topples over. The water hits him. He splutters and coughs; his lungs fill. The water is freezing; it knocks the air out of his body and now it is closing over his head. He feels himself sinking . . . sinking . . . his clothes dragging him down.

❧§ 21 ❧

SOPHIA

Put a curb upon thy desires if thou wouldst not fall into some disorder.

Jacob Cats quoting Aristotle

I get home only just in time. In the kitchen I hang up Maria's shawl and cap – she is asleep – and bundle her clothes back into the chest. Thank God there are no other servants in the house. Just then, far off, I hear the front door slam.

I race upstairs in my chemise. It is dark up here. Gasping for breath I bang against the doorpost, steady myself and blunder into the bedchamber.

Downstairs I hear Cornelis lock the front door. I stand there, frozen with fear, my lover's seed sliding down my thigh. Blinded by sin, I feel for the bedpost.

I make it just in time. I hear my husband's step. Candle-light flickers on the wall as he ascends the stairs. And by the time he comes in I am under the covers, curled up, my arms around my knees.

❦§ 22 ❧❦

WILLEM

*The foam of water shows itself to be of lesser whiteness the
further down it is from the surface of the water, and this is
proved [because] ... the natural colour of something
submerged will be the more transformed into the green
colour of the water to the extent that the thing submerged
has a greater quantity of water above it.*

Leonardo da Vinci, *Notebooks*

For a moment Willem does not struggle. He surrenders
himself to the water. He watches himself drowning; his
soul has already detached itself. Memories swim up – his
mother's face, with its whiskery mole; his sister
sniggering, and pressing her hand to her mouth ... He
knows he is dying and he welcomes extinction, for do we
not bloom sweetly, for just a season, and then perish?
Wherever he goes God is there, ready to take him into
His arms.

Willem sinks, a piece of flotsam thrown out by this
city, he and the dead dogs and meat bones. He drifts
down, he and the contents of the nightpots of a hundred
and twenty thousand men and women.

Unlike most of the city's inhabitants, however, Willem
can swim. Why he wants to live when everything – his
bride, his hopes, his fortune – has been stolen from him;
why his rude instinct for survival fights against his desire
for oblivion – he has no time to answer, for he is battling

his way to the surface and now he splashes and flails, gasping for breath. He swims to the side and claws at the slimy wall. The water slops him bumpingly against the brickwork. He gropes his way along it until he fumbles against a mooring ring. He clings to it, coughing up the water from his lungs. And finally he hoists himself out – how heavy he weighs: the dead weight of a mortal after all. He lies in the street, sodden.

The next morning, battered, bruised and with nothing to live for, Willem packs his bags and makes his way down to the docks. Here he enlists in the navy and within a few days his ship has set sail to fight the Spanish, the last fightable foe left to him and a more patriotic focus for his rage.

✂§ 23 §✂

JAN

Take linseed and dry it in a pan, without water, on the fire. Put it in a mortar and pound it to a fine powder; then replacing it in the pan and pouring a little water on it, make it quite hot. Afterwards wrap it in a piece of new linen; place it in a press used for extracting the oil of olives, of walnuts, and express this in the same manner. With this oil grind minium or vermilion, or any other colour you wish, on a stone slab ... prepare tints for faces and draperies ... distinguishing, according to your fancy, animals, birds, or foliage with their proper colours.

Theophilus, 11th century

Jan is feeling guilty about the boy. He has been too distracted to give him much attention. Jacob has been grinding pigments for him and cleaning brushes – humble jobs; otherwise he has only had a few drawing lessons. The boy has talent; he draws with greater skill than Jan possessed at his age and he is keen to learn. Jacob is less moody than Jan, too; less tempestuous. Jan cannot picture him falling catastrophically in love with one of his sitters. One day he will make a good living as a competent, workmanlike painter. Not great, maybe, but who says Jan will be great? Not Mattheus. *You have to be courageous, my friend, and unafraid of pain.*

So Jan sets his pupil down in front of the double portrait and tells him to finish painting Cornelis – the hands, the spindly, old-man's shins. Jan cannot bring himself to paint the legs that have lain between Sophia's thighs. He has painted the old man's face, but he has only sketched in the rest; he doesn't want anything else to do with him.

Sophia is finished but she is a Sophia who is long since gone. For ever she will sit demurely beside her husband but the real woman, like a ghost, has since risen and come to him. For the first time in his life Jan's professionalism has deserted him. He cannot bear to carry on; the painting is dead. He will help the boy with the background and then it will be finished.

For he is absorbed in another painting. It is called *The Love Letter*.

Describe the room where you read my letter, he asked her.

In the bedchamber ... panelled walls, waxed and polished cabinet. A tapestry behind me, 'Orpheus in the Underworld' ... the bed – no, he's not going to paint the bed.

What were you wearing?

My violet silk dress, you have not seen it. Black bodice stitched with velvet and silver.

What were thinking?

I was thinking: the world has stopped ... my heart is going to burst ...

With happiness? he asked.

With fear.

Don't be afraid, my love.

I was thinking: all my life I have been asleep and now I have opened my eyes. I was thinking: he loves me too! I felt as if my body had turned to water. (How is he going to paint that?) *I was thinking – do I dare? I kept leaving the house and then stopping. I didn't dare.*

Ah, but you did, he said, kissing her fingers.

He loves Sophia for her recklessness – a maid's disguise! He loves her for her spirit and ingenuity. She is a woman after his own heart.

I was thinking what it would be like to kiss you, she said. *And I hated you for making me mock my husband – oh I am all confused!*

Sophia is here in his studio. She is always with him, he talks to her in his head. He sees her standing at the window reading the letter. All painting is illusion. Sophia, though absent, stands here more breathingly real than the solid sitters he has painted in the past. Art lies, to tell the truth. Flowers from different seasons bloom impossibly together. Trees are shifted around in the landscape to frame the composition. Rooms are created like stage sets, furnished with the artist's own possessions, where models are arranged in a speechless moment of drama. Even straight portraits are only an approximation, filtered through the painter's eye. Their realism, down to the tiniest detail – this too is a deception.

In the foreground, on the table, Jan has arranged a still life from his own collection – goblets and jewellery he keeps in the chest for this purpose. They are not hers, just as this room is not hers, but in the painting they will belong to her. Nor do they have any moral message – no skull, no empty mussel shells, no open lantern lying on the floor. They are simply things of beauty that will exist for this moment, in this painting. They are simply there to celebrate his love.

Later that day Sophia visits. She slips in for an hour, on her way home from doing some errands. She wears the violet dress for him; he has asked her to do this. They don't kiss – Jacob is here, whistling as he paints. Gerrit is banging around in the kitchen.

It's a sunny afternoon. Sophia stands at the window. The light bathes her face. Jan gives her another letter to read, for they cannot speak openly.

She looks at the paper. *You are my life. Come to me and spend the night. I want to hold you in my arms and feel you dreaming. I will love you until I die.*

As she reads it she stiffens. He sketches her quickly, with charcoal. She reads it again and turns to him.

'Don't look at me,' he says. 'Read it again – your head, just like that.'

Jacob stops whistling. He is listening to them.

Sophia's lips twitch. She says: 'I'll read it aloud.'

Jan stares at her. 'Is that wise?'

She reads: '*Dear Cornelis Sandvoort, your picture is nearing completion. It will be ready for delivery this Tuesday next. I trust it will meet with your approval and look forward to the final settlement of my fee at your pleasure.*'

Behind his hand, Jan snorts with laughter. Sophia remains gazing out of the window.

Jacob asks: 'What is this painting to be called?'

'*The Love Letter*,' replies Jan.

'*Love* letter?' says his pupil. 'It doesn't sound like one to me.'

'All painting is deception,' says Jan. 'Haven't you learnt that yet?'

Sophia chuckles. Jan turns back to his drawing.

A smell of cooking drifts in from the next room. Just for a moment there is a feeling of domesticity – Jacob whistling, Gerrit in the kitchen. Gerrit is a terrible cook

– Jan usually prepares food himself or goes out to eat – but today it smells delicious. It is all an illusion, of course. Sophia will not eat the *hutspot*, she will soon be gone. She should not be here in the first place – she has put herself at great risk by coming to his studio in broad daylight.

But what is reality? This feels utterly real and utterly right. Through lies, he is painting the truth. He has reassembled a life here for her and look how radiant she is! She stands there rereading the letter. When she is gone the radiance will remain.

Jan works fast. He feels alive – thrilled to his fingertips and it is not just desire, it is something more. So much of the time he feels that he is just putting paint on to canvas. Now he is truly working.

❧ 24 ❧

Sophia

Run not therefore East or West,
Home for girls is much the best.

Jacob Cats, *Moral Emblems*, 1632

I feel absurdly joyful – carefree, in fact – as I step out of Jan's studio. The street is empty; nobody has seen me. A pied cat streaks past. This, I decide, is a good omen. I create omens to suit myself; I am not like Maria, in thrall to the old superstitions. I am released from that, I have broken the rules, and look – nobody has found me out. Those loading doors, high up in that warehouse – I have stepped out of them and see, I didn't fall. I flew! I have been given the airy immunity of an angel.

It is a glorious sunny afternoon; spring has truly arrived. *Come to me and spend the night.* I love Jan to distraction. I know I should feel guilty but I have shut down that part of myself. I am a carriage, being pulled by galloping horses even though my wheels are locked rigid. The wheels are my faith. I am powerless. Punishment awaits me but not yet, not now.

This is how I feel today as I walk past the flower seller (hyacinths; shiny blue in the sunshine); past the front doors (shiny green). I learnt this locking-off technique when my father beat me. I shut myself off from my body and my spirit flew free, I could watch myself with detachment. It hurt, of course, but it did not matter.

I have not thought about my father for a long time; I have not thought about anybody. Love has made me self-absorbed. I loved my father and he loved me; he only hit me when he was drunk. He was a passionate man who, disappointed in life, took refuge in wine. When he died I was devastated. Maybe that was why I sought an older man, or allowed myself to be claimed. I was fourteen when he passed away. I thought – if God loves me, why does He give me such pain? It was God's will, of course, that my father died, but why did it feel like a betrayal?

I couldn't ask these questions aloud so I shut them away. Ours is a tolerant country; Catholics and Calvinists live together, as I live with my husband. Whatever our faith, however, it is deeply rooted, it is the very foundation of our existence. We live in the presence of God. The glory of this day – the sun, the bunches of hyacinths – belongs to Him and our celebration of beauty is all in His name. I mock this at my peril.

For I am in mortal danger. The sun lulls me with its warmth, my heart sings. I truly believe I can keep my secret safe. On Saturday my husband is attending a banquet given by the Civic Guard; he will get drunk and come home late. I will slip away and spend the evening with my lover, he and I have planned it. If Maria is sleeping I will borrow her clothes again. She is sleeping a lot lately – dozing during the day, falling asleep as soon as her work is finished. I wonder, in a dreamy way, what is the matter with her. Then my dreams revert back to myself. How happy I am – how blindly happy.

For ahead of me lies the drop – and I really believed I could fly.

*

Maria is sitting in the kitchen chopping onions. The place is a mess – the fire is dead, vegetable peelings and unwashed cooking pots lie on the floor. I have not entered the kitchen today – this morning I had a singing lesson and I have been out all afternoon.

Maria, too, must have left the house earlier. Her cloak lies in a heap on the floor. The cat sleeps on it, bathed in a pool of sunlight. Maria looks at me. Her face is streaming with tears. For a moment I think it's caused by the onions.

'Have you finished the ironing?' I ask.

'Madam, I've got something to tell you.' Her face crumples. 'I'm going to have a baby.'

I have poured her some brandy. She gulps it down.

'I trusted him! I thought he wanted to marry me. He said he wanted to make an honest woman of me.'

'Where is he?'

'I was worried what had happened to him, it's not like Willem, see –'

'What's happened to him?'

'He's gone,' she wails. 'I went down to the fish market this morning, I hadn't seen him for days.' She takes another gulp. 'He promised to marry me.'

'Where is he, Maria?'

'I don't know. He sold up his share in the business – he had this partnership with his friend – a week ago he sold it up and one morning he just didn't turn up at the market. He's gone. Nobody knows where.' She bursts into sobs. 'He's left me. I thought he loved me! I don't know what to do and now I'm going to have his baby.'

The cat opens its pink mouth and yawns. It rises from the crumpled cloak and stalks off.

'How could he do that to you?' I ask. 'Did he know you're . . .'

She shakes her head.

'You don't know where he has gone? What about his family?'

'They live in Friesland.' Maria's nose is running; her hair has escaped from its cap and falls around her face. She sits slumped in the chair.

'You must find him and marry him.'

'But I don't know where to look! He's left me, he doesn't want me –'

'But if he knows you're carrying his child –'

'He has gone! Don't you understand, miss? He's gone.'

She looks plain, her face as heavy as dough. I lean down awkwardly and hug her.

'Oh my poor girl,' I say.

The cat rubs itself against our legs.

I am all disordered. I should be feeling sorry for Maria – I do feel pity for her – but I am also trembling on my own behalf. I myself could fall pregnant – might easily do so. The father could be either of the two men – would I pass the baby off as my husband's? Maria is carrying the results of my own iniquity. How easily this could be me, and what would be the consequences then? A greater hand is at work, arranging our fates. A greater power has been observing me, and has punished my own maid for my sins.

I sit on my bed, trying to sort out my thoughts. I hear Maria's footsteps on the stairs. They already sound heavier. She should be preparing the evening meal – I should be supervising her – for soon Cornelis will be home and will wonder what has happened. There is a trapped, static atmosphere in the house; he will guess that something is wrong.

Maria enters without tapping on the door. She sits down next to me on the bed. Such familiarity startles me, but then she is upset.

'My poor girl.' I stroke her hand – how chapped it is. 'You must go home.'

'Home?' She stares at me. 'I cannot go home. The shame!'

'But you must –'

'My father will kill me!'

'Surely not –'

'You don't know him,' she says sharply.

'My father had a quick temper too – but surely, in the end, he will forgive you?'

'He will kill me.' There's a dull finality in her voice. 'What else do you suggest, madam? That I have the child aborted? That I drown it at birth? That I take to the streets, a disgraced woman, an outcast, that I die of shame and starvation?' Raising her head, she says: 'Please let me stay here.'

'You can't, Maria, you know that's impossible.'

'Are you going to throw me out?'

'Of course you can stay on here for a few more weeks, but –'

'Just tell me, are you going to throw me out?'

What does one do in these circumstances? I have no idea. 'When my husband hears of it you will have no choice. You simply cannot remain here, Maria, you know that.'

She takes a breath and looks at me. Her eyes narrow to slits. 'If you throw me out I'll tell your husband what you have been up to.'

There is a silence.

'What did you say?' I ask.

'You heard.'

I cannot speak. I'm falling – falling through space.

She says: 'I'll tell him, miss. I've got nothing to lose.'

My throat has closed. I cannot meet her eye; I stare into the huge mouth of the hearth: the dead grate, the tarred bricks behind. I will it to swallow me up.

At last I say: 'How do you know?'

'I'm not stupid.'

'How?'

'That letter you tore up – I read it. Didn't even need to read it. I could tell, when he was here, you and him.'

'You could tell?' I whisper.

'And I wasn't asleep that night. I saw you hanging up my cloak, I put two and two together. I wouldn't have spoken, I'm not that sort, but if you're going to be like this.' She smooths down her apron, setting herself to rights. 'So don't get all lofty with me.' She gets to her feet. 'If we sink, we sink together.'

CORNELIS

If man is the head, then the woman is the neck upon which it rests.

17th-century household manual

On Sundays Cornelis enjoys fetching his wife from her place of worship, Our Lord in the Attic, a private Catholic dwelling near the Oude Kerk. He likes to walk home through the streets of his fair city – such beauty, such prosperity! – with Sophia on his arm. After a week's hard work, it is his reward. Men gaze at him with envy; he swells with pride. Acquaintances stop to greet him. It is a public display of his miraculous good fortune.

On a sunny day like this the whole population seems to be on the streets – respectable burghers and their wives, tradespeople in their Sunday best. Church-going has purified them; they have repented their sins and been made whole, they have been saved from eternal damnation. They move like a black wave through the streets. Their souls are as scrubbed clean as the doorsteps along the way; their faith is as shiny as the door knockers. How clean is his nation, scoured both within and without! Foreigners marvel at the polish.

On Sundays Cornelis feels his past more keenly. This morning, as always, he prayed for the souls of his sons, Frans and Pieter, and his first wife. On weekdays, at home, Sophia kneels at his side; he feels constrained by her presence. On Sundays, however, their faiths separate them; kneeling alone, he feels freer to commune with his lost family. Jesus has gathered up his sons to His bosom; they are in heaven, preserved for ever as infants sprouting wings.

This is what he tells himself. Recently, however, he has felt a disturbing sensation. His sons are simply small corpses, senselessly snuffed out. That is all. Beyond that is emptiness. Sometimes, sitting in his hard pew – *I believe in God the Father* – sometimes, sitting there, Cornelis is gripped by terror. There is no heaven, only a spilled deck of cards. Life is a gamble, it is nothing but a handful of tulip bulbs, a brace of kings. Even the righteous can draw the joker from the pack.

He can tell nobody this – certainly not Sophia. It would disturb her, to voice these demons of doubt. His wife is an innocent young woman, steadfast in her faith. It would be as unthinkable as telling her about Grietje lifting her skirts. For it was God's will that his sons were taken from him and to question this is blasphemy.

Cornelis has a new life now and a new young wife. She is younger than his sons would be, had they survived. Their ghosts walk beside him. Their unlived years have made them tall and strong. Their unmet spouses and unborn children are somewhere here, at the edges of his vision. The air echoes, like the silence after bells have ceased tolling – it echoes with stopped possibilities. His sons are speaking to him, their faces sorrowful with pity, and they are telling him the truth although he tries to block his ears. *There is nothing there, believe us.* Sophia must not hear. All Cornelis's dreams are packed into her, like flower petals packed into a bud. She is his only hope now, for his future simply lies here, on this temporal earth.

The question is – when will the bud burst into blossom? For despite all his efforts Sophia still does not conceive. The night before, when he returned from the banquet, he laboured between her legs. She lay there mutely, holding him as he shuddered. Silently he implored God to make his seed fruitful. Afterwards, however, he heard her sobbing – noiseless sobs, deep in the pillow when she had presumed he was sleeping. She too wanted a child. *My God, my God, why hast Thou forsaken me?*

The streets are full of children today, walking home from church. A boy, holding his mother's hand, turns to gaze at a pigeon. Twin girls, sucking twin thumbs, look down at their feet and try to walk in step. Amsterdam is filled with families – his ghost family within his head and real families in rude health. They taunt him with their happiness.

Cornelis is a man of routine. Every Sunday he buys Sophia a pancake, dusted with sugar, at the stall in the Dam. They stop there; he breathes the aroma of vanilla and almonds. A small boy pulls at his father's arm, urging him to buy. He has flaxen curls, like a cherub, and ruddy cheeks painted by Rubens. Cornelis's heart shifts beneath his ribs.

Sophia has not said a word. She has been quiet all day. Maybe she is thinking the same thing. Cornelis passes her a pancake, wrapped in a twist of paper. He gestures round at the sunlit scene. 'What a beautiful day. I seek only one thing to make my happiness complete.'

Sophia, the pancake half-way to her mouth, stares at him. She looks as if she has woken from a dream.

She pauses for a moment, then she takes a bite.

❦ 26 ❦

SOPHIA

Good pictures are very common here, there being scarce an ordinary tradesman whose house is not adorned with them.

William Aglionby, *The Present State of the Low Countries*, 1669

Gerrit, Jan's servant, opens the door and lets us in. My husband and I step into the studio. Jan stands beside the finished painting.

I am sweating – my palms, my armpits. I didn't want to come here but Cornelis insisted and my refusal might have struck him as curious.

'Would you care for a glass of wine?' asks Jan, addressing my husband.

Cornelis is an intruder into my secret life. Surely he can sense that I have been here? The bed looms up; it seems abnormally large, standing in the corner of the room, its curtains closed. It draws the eye with a magnetic force.

Cornelis looks around. What if I have left something here, something that he will recognize? Even with no evidence the room is filled with my presence. He must surely feel it, that this is my true home now, that my heart is here.

Gerrit brings us *roemers* of wine on a tray – the best glasses. I sip, looking at Jan over the rim. He has greeted me politely; our eyes have barely met. If he is as nervous as I am he is keeping it well hidden.

'Does the painting meet with your approval, sir?' he asks.

Cornelis steps close to the canvas – he is short-sighted. He nods and murmurs to himself.

The pupil, Jacob, points. 'It is finely rendered, is it not? Your legs in particular, don't you think? Regard the brushwork.'

Cornelis nods. 'Very fine. My dear, do you like it?'

My hand trembles as I hold the glass. They are all watching me. Jacob has a pale, intelligent face; he misses nothing. Gerrit's lumpy peasant's face is like a potato. In their different ways they are both dangerous. Will they betray me? Yet I am also filled with tenderness for them; they belong to this place, they are included in my love.

I start to speak, but Cornelis interrupts me. 'Oh but I look old!' he says. 'I am but sixty-one yet I look an old man – is this how the world sees me?' He turns to me with a thin smile. 'We should call this painting *Winter and Spring*.'

'I paint what I see,' says Jan shortly. 'Nothing more and nothing less.'

'You have certainly caught *her* beauty.' Cornelis turns to me. 'The bloom on her cheeks, her freshness and youth like the dew on a peach. Who was it – Karel van Mander? Who, on seeing a still life tried to reach into the canvas and pluck the fruit?' He clears his throat. 'Not realizing that this particular peach was not to be eaten.'

There is a silence. Outside, a bell chimes the hour. Does Cornelis suspect something?

'I will have the painting delivered to your house

tomorrow,' says Jan, taking our empty *roemers*. He looks uncomfortable; he is longing for us to leave.

But I must speak to him. I must tell him about Maria's pregnancy and the idea that has been brewing in my mind – an idea so bold, so breath-taking that I hardly dare put it into words. Now is not the time, for Jan is ushering us to the door. It pains me that I cannot kiss him goodbye.

As I pass him I whisper: 'I have a plan.'

'What did you say?'

Maria stares at me, her eyes as round as platters. All day she has been dozy but now she is wide awake. We are in the parlour. Above her hangs a canvas of a slaughtered hare; it is my least favourite painting in the house. Hooked up by its bleeding hind leg, the hare hangs upside down. Its eye, glazed by death, rests on us with indifference as I tell her my plan.

Maria claps her hand to her mouth. 'But, madam – but you can't!'

'*I* can, but what about you?'

'But . . . but . . .' Her voice trails away. My robust, chatty maid – for once she is silent.

Then her face breaks into a grin. She sits there under the sacrificial hare – a pitiful, furry *Descent from the Cross* – and shakes with appalled laughter.

❧ 27 ❧

CORNELIS

You must cultivate the infertile land so that it can bear
* fruit,*
Dig, uproot, make trenches,
Pull out the weeds, from the very first day,
So that your esteemed husband can sow there afterwards.

Jacob Cats, 1625

'*And the flood was forty days upon the earth; and the waters*
increased, and bare up the ark, and it was lift up above the
earth . . . and all flesh died that moved upon the earth, both of
fowl, and of cattle, and of beast and of every creeping thing that
creepeth upon the earth, and every man . . . all in whose nostrils
was the breath of life, of all that was on the dry land, died . . .'

Cornelis is reading to his wife. This chapter in Genesis
always stirs him. His country, too, was once drowned.
Floods engulfed the land but with God's will the people
of Holland reclaimed it from the sea; they redeemed it
and created an earthly paradise – fertile soil, fair cities, a
peaceful and tolerant country where faiths could mingle,
Mennonite and Catholic, Protestant and Jew, the lion
lying down beside the lamb. How fortunate they are, and
how especially fortunate he is.

Sophia's head is bent over her sewing; she is darning a
bedsheet. The oil lamp shines on her soft brown hair,
curly at the temples, coiled at the nape of her neck. Their
portrait now hangs on the wall; it was delivered

yesterday. The picture seals their union. And his business is flourishing. He has shares in several ships. This month a fleet of two hundred vessels is setting sail for the Baltic; from there they will carry grain to southern Europe. In August a fleet of twenty ships is due to return from the East Indies laden with spices, ivory and two hundred tons of gold apiece. If God grants them a safe passage Cornelis will make a substantial profit.

'And God remembered Noah, and every living thing, and all the cattle that was with him in the ark; and God made a wind to pass over the earth, and the waters assuaged . . . and Noah removed the covering of the ark, and looked, and behold, the face of the ground was dry.'

Cornelis closes the Bible. It is time for bed. Later, he remembers this evening as one of profound contentment. It is as if he already senses the joy to come.

For in bed, when he lays his hand on Sophia's breast she gently removes it.

'My dear,' she says. 'I have some news that I know will please you as much as it delights me.' She strokes his fingers. 'I visited the physician today and he confirmed what I have suspected. I am carrying your child.'

❧ 28 ❧

SOPHIA

Except the Lord built the house, their labour is but lost that built it. Except the Lord keep the city, the watchman waketh but in vain.

Psalm 127

When I was little there was a picture that gave me nightmares. Back in Utrecht, where I grew up, my father owned a print shop. Our front room served as the shop; it opened on to the street where, under the canopy, more prints were displayed. Below street level, downstairs in the vault, that was where the printing press thrummed and clattered. My father printed pamphlets and leaflets – moral verses, sermons and edifying works recommended by the predicants: *The Threshold of Paradise*, *The Delight of Piety*. He also printed etchings and engravings of paintings.

The one that haunted me was pinned to the wall – perhaps it haunted him too, I never asked. It was a print of the great flood of 1421, the St Elizabeth's Day flood that drowned whole villages for ever. The picture shows an expanse of water. Poking through the surface are tree-tops and the spires of churches. The water has swallowed them up.

I gazed at it for hours – the stillness of the water, the tips of the spires, the horrors that lay beneath. God had saved Noah; why did these people deserve to be damned? I heard the bells tolling, calling drowned men to worship. Way below were bloated cattle with sightless eyes; they moved in the current, bumping against the roofs of barns. In one convulsion the world had been turned upside down. Deep in the water the dead moved helplessly. Their arms waved like weeds, but nobody came to their rescue.

Jan stares at me. 'The Lord preserve us! You really intend doing this?'

We are sitting on the rim of a water fountain, a few streets from his house. His neighbourhood is full of artisans' workshops – carpenters, goldsmiths, painters. Beside us there is a metalworker's premises. Hammer blows ring out. We meet in the open because it is less risky than me being seen going into his house. Maria, our look-out, stands at the end of the alley. She is my partner now. *If we sink, we sink together.*

'Surely he will notice?' asks Jan. 'He will notice that Maria's getting fatter?'

'She's a big girl. The difference will scarcely be discernible, if she wears her apron higher.'

'But surely –'

'My husband is short-sighted,' I reply breezily. 'He never looks at her anyway – she is a servant, she is simply an item of furniture.'

'But what about you? How are *you* going to grow bigger?' Jan looks shaken. He seems to be more nervous than I am. 'He will notice *you*.'

'I'll feign the symptoms. After a few months I'll stuff a pillow down my dress –'

'But he's your husband, he shares your bed, surely

he'll discover you –'

'Ah, that is the beauty of my plan. You know that I cannot bear him touching me. I cannot bear . . .' I stop. 'I told him that from now until my confinement we have been forbidden conjugal relations. The doctor ordered it, for my health. I'm delicate, you understand.'

'Are you?'

'And my husband would do anything not to lose the baby. I said we must have separate beds, so I can rest undisturbed, and he agreed. He's so happy he will agree to anything.'

Jan shakes his head wonderingly. He takes my hand. 'You are an extraordinary woman.'

Just desperate. I'm desperate for him. 'It means Maria can stay on, in our employment. This device suits both of us – she helps me and I help her . . .'

What then? I have not yet considered that. I am too thrilled with my plan to think beyond my phantom pregnancy, which is becoming so real that I'm almost feeling sick. After all, my husband believes it; this makes it half-way real already.

'But what happens if you too fall pregnant?' he asks.

'Then we have to change the plan.'

Jan starts laughing helplessly. He puts his arms around me and kisses me, in broad daylight. After all, what could be more reckless than what I have set in motion?

Hammer blows ring out, sealing our fate.

I know I should be angry with Maria, for blackmailing me and forcing this bold plan into action. She too is terrified that something should go wrong and we will be found out. But I am also profoundly grateful to her, more

grateful than she will ever know. She has released me from my marital bed. I have borne my husband's love-making for three years and would no doubt have borne it until he died, but since I've met my lover Cornelis has become so repulsive to me that I have felt violated – his sour breath; his cold, probing fingers. Worse than that – I have felt like a whore.

Miraculously, a solution has presented itself. It is one that will benefit Maria too, for though she has behaved ruthlessly I am fond of her. She is my only friend and I am glad to save her from poverty and ostracism.

What will happen in the future? Neither of us thinks of that. We are young, we have acted on impulse, we have stepped into a world of deceit, but so far we just feel like schoolchildren who have managed to trick our teacher and get away with it.

Are we not blind? Are we not reckless? We are two desperate young women; we are in love. And love, as we know, is a form of madness.

Maria and I are making up a bed for Cornelis in the room opposite mine. It is called the Leather Room; he sometimes uses it as a study. It is chilly in here, but then all our rooms are chilly. The walls are lined with stamped leather; dark landscapes hang there, views by Hans Bols and Gillis van Coninxloo. There is a heavy cupboard crammed with porcelain jars from China.

As we plump up the pillows Cornelis comes in. He strokes his beard. 'It is a small price to pay,' he says. He is so happy, it should break my heart. 'Let Maria do that,' he says. 'You must look after yourself.'

Suddenly Maria clutches her stomach. With a heaving

grunt she rushes out. She is going to vomit. She has been vomiting all week.

I hastily follow her into what is now my bedchamber and close the door. Maria grabs the nightpot, just in time, and vomits noisily into it. I stand behind her, supporting her head in my hands and stroking her forehead.

When she is finished we hear a tap at the door. 'Are you all right, my dear?' calls Cornelis.

Maria and I look at each other. Quick as a flash she shoves the pot into my hands.

Cornelis comes in. He takes one look at the vessel – there is a foul smell – and says: 'My poor dearest.'

'It is only natural, in the first months,' I reply. 'It is a small price to pay.'

I carry the pot to the door. He stops me. 'Let the maid do that.' He glares at Maria. 'Maria!'

I hand Maria the pot. Eyes lowered, she takes it from me and carries it downstairs.

And so begin the strangest months of my life. Looking back, from beyond my death, I see a woman hurtling downstream on the current, as helpless as a twig. She is too young to think where she is going; she is too blind with passion to think about tomorrow. Someone might betray her; she knows this is only too possible. She might even betray herself. God waits in judgement. He is the one she has most profoundly betrayed. But she locks that muscle in her heart. Not now, she thinks. Not yet.

I have invented a doctor – a man recommended by my singing teacher, whom Cornelis has never met. My husband is anxious about my condition; he wants his own physician to attend me but I've persuaded him otherwise. He bends to my every wish. He humours me; he treats me like a precious piece of Wan-Li porcelain.

In these early weeks Maria craves cloves. I tell Cornelis of my craving. He brings home marzipan pastries, flavoured with cloves. Maria devours them in the kitchen. He orders Maria to prepare *hippocras* – spiced wine made with cloves – and watches me fondly as I drink. Alone in the kitchen Maria drinks the dregs.

For I do, in fact, almost believe it myself. After all, I am a woman; I have been created for motherhood. Since girlhood I have been brought up with this in mind and my condition seems so natural, after three years of marriage, that I can almost convince myself it is real. As the weeks pass I am discovering in myself a capacity for self-deception. This in itself is not surprising; since I have become an adulteress I have learnt how to dissemble. I have become an actress in the most dangerous theatre of all – my home. And I have not yet reached the stage of all-too-solid deceit – strapping a pillow around my waist – I have not yet faced that. This phantom pregnancy, so far, is an abstraction – nausea and a craving for cloves.

Maria and I are close – closer than I have been to my sisters, close in a way nobody else could comprehend. Only Jan knows our secret. Maria suffers from sickness – not in the mornings but later in the day. I hear her retching in the kitchen and run in to hold her clammy forehead. I feel responsible for her convulsions, as if I have caused them; I feel it should be me who suffers. In fact, I do feel nauseous, too.

She is carrying my child and our complicity binds us

together. We are locked in this house with our secret. These silent rooms, bathed in light through the coloured glass – they guard our treachery. Our only witnesses are the faces that gaze from the paintings – King David; a peasant raising a tankard; our own selves, Cornelis and me, posed in our former life. These are our mute collaborators.

When we're alone, our positions are reversed. I look after Maria; I am *her* servant. If she is tired I put her to bed in the wall; I scour the cooking pots and sweep the floor before my husband returns. 'Polish the candle-sticks,' she bosses, 'he always notices.'

To the outside world, however, she is my servant and I am a pregnant wife. Cornelis, the proud father-to-be, has told the news to our friends and acquaintances. Blushing, I have accepted their congratulations. Our neighbour Mrs Molenaer has sent around a herbal infusion to ease my sickness. 'It will disappear after three months,' she says. 'It always does.'

I give it to Maria, who drinks it. She says it makes her feel even worse. Later Mrs Molenaer visits and asks if I am feeling better. 'Oh yes,' I reply as Maria, her face grey, serves us pastries. But who notices a servant?

'When is the confinement?' asks Mrs Molenaer. 'When is the happy day?'

'In November.'

'Your family lives in Utrecht, am I right? They must be very happy at the news.'

'Oh, they are.'

'Will your mother attend the birth?'

'My mother is unwell. I doubt that she could under-take the journey.'

Why so many questions? They make me nervous. A woman in my condition is the focus of attention; I hope it will not last. I feel a cheat, of course, as if I have copied out someone else's verse and been praised for writing it myself. I need all my energies to keep my wits. My family, for instance. Cornelis believes that I have sent a letter to my mother and sisters, telling them the happy news. Out of cowardice I have put this off. I will have to pretend, at some point, that I have received a reply. And soon he will be expecting at least one of my sisters to visit – after all, Utrecht is but twenty-five miles distant. Luckily he is out most of the day, at his warehouse in the harbour. I shall have to concoct a visit while he is at work.

It is the strangest sensation, that Maria is pregnant with my baby. I have stepped into the world of motherhood and I am now noticing children in the street, gazing at them with a maternal interest. In our country we show affection to our offspring; in fact, foreigners remark that we treat them with excessive indulgence. Rather than being consigned to the care of nursemaids, our Dutch children are brought up in the bosom of the family. Opposite my front door, across the canal, the houses catch the sunlight in the morning. A woman brings her child outside. She watches it take its first steps. Along the street the trees are misted green; new life is beginning. She swoops the child up and holds it close. I can hear her laughter, echoing across the canal. This affects me deeply. She is my phantom self with my phantom child. This is the lost life that I should have been leading with my husband. Treacherous water, however, separates us, and I cannot reach her now.

'Lord, this is heavy!' Indoors Maria attempts to lift a bucket of peat. I take it from her. She giggles. I know she is using me but I do not mind. She must not lose this baby. She is not being attended by a doctor; she only has me. While I have all the attention she has to cope alone. And it is she who will face, alone, the unimaginable terrors of childbirth. Sometimes, burdened with my lies, I forget this. There is danger ahead for both of us, but only she will bear the pain.

I empty the peat into the box beside the fireplace. My arms ache – it is hard work, being a servant. 'Feel my *tieten* – they're getting bigger.' Maria is two months gone. Ignoring my blushes, she grabs my hand and lays it on her breast. I have never felt her before, so I cannot tell. Besides, she is a buxom girl.

'There's storks nesting on the chimney down the road,' she says. 'That's good luck.' She is drinking some concoction of cow's urine and dung, she buys it from an old woman in the market. She is in thrall to country superstitions – around her neck she wears a charm: a walnut shell with a spider's head inside, to ward off fever. Before, I would have laughed at this – I come from a middle-class, educated family; we were taught to ridicule such things – but now she has drawn me into her world. I want to believe her magic, for only a miracle will see us through. We are bound together by sorcery.

It is May. The evenings are balmy. On warm days the canals stink, but over them drifts the scent of blossoms. In the gardens, tulips sound their silent trumpets; irises have unfurled between their swords. Even the house seems pregnant with new life. On the wall hangs Cornelis's lute, swollen like a fruit; on the kitchen shelves stand the big-bellied stoneware jars.

Released from Cornelis's embraces, my passion for Jan grows stronger. I surrender myself to him with my whole heart. Nowadays I visit his studio in broad daylight. Of course I am careful, I make sure nobody sees me slipping through the door. My hood hides my face. But I have grown in confidence. My great deception has made me reckless. One huge lie and I have stepped over a threshold into another world; a criminal must feel this, after he has killed for the first time. And look! I have got away with it. Nobody has found me out, not yet. There is no going back now, I am caught in the momentum of my crime. I feel exhilarated by my wicked success.

Jan shuts his pupil into the kitchen. He has set up a still life for Jacob there, an *ontbijtje* or breakfast table – half-eaten ham, earthenware mustard pot, grapes. Jacob wants to add a butterfly – 'To symbolize the carefree life of the soul,' he says, 'after it is free from fleshly desires.'

'Just paint a breakfast,' says Jan.

'What about a peeled lemon, so beautiful, yet sour inside?'

'Just look at what's on the table,' says Jan. 'Look at the lustre of the grapes. Isn't that enough? Find beauty in what you see, not what it can teach us.'

Jacob is an earnest young man. How can he detach objects from their sermonizing properties? To paint earthly beauty, just for itself, is to deny the presence of God. Jacob already considers Jan disreputable. He knows there is something going on between us, and me a married woman. Ah, what would he think if he knew the truth?

Jan closes the door on his pupil. He is going to paint me. He has finished *The Love Letter*. I smuggled it into the house and hid it in the attic. That was his love letter to me, one I will never tear up. Now, in his studio, he paints me naked. I disrobe myself, peeling off my clothes like an onion skin. But the tears in my eyes are caused by happiness.

'Shall I tell you how much I love you?' I ask, lying on the bed. 'When I see a leek, my heart leaps. Do you know why?'

'Why, my sweetest heart, my darling love? Move your arm up – there, just like that.'

'Because I was drinking leek soup when I first heard your name. *Jan van Loos, he will make me immortal.*'

'And I will! Leave your husband, Sophia, come and live with me.'

'How can I leave my husband when I am carrying his child?' I laugh.

Jan is shocked. How can I talk so lightly? 'Sooner or later you'll be found out, it's only a matter of time.'

'Why should I be found out?'

'What's going to happen when the child is born? Are you going to pass it off as your own and go on living with your husband?'

I cannot contemplate this. I cannot bear to think about the future.

'What are we going to do,' he asks, 'now we have started this?'

'If I run away with you, he'll discover I have been cheating. Besides, where can we go? We cannot stay here and if we move to another town you will be unable to work, your guild forbids it.' This is true. To protect their members, the Guilds of St Luke are closed to painters from other towns; they are unable to sell their work until they've been established there for several years.

Now it is Jan's turn to be reckless. 'We'll leave the country. We'll sail to the East Indies.'

'The East Indies?'

'We'll escape from this life and start again, you and I – we'll sail across the world and nobody will be able to reach us.' He clasps me in his arms. 'My love, we'll be happy.'

So the seed is sown. Jan talks about sunshine and ultramarine skies. 'Mountains – can you picture them?' He has heard travellers' tales of the colony. 'And trees chattering with parrots. The sun shines all the year round. We won't need money – besides, what happiness has money brought you? We will lie as naked as God intended under the palm trees and I will rub your beautiful long body with myrrh.'

At this stage it is still a dream – as foreign as the exotic prints my father used to show me. Too many obstacles lie in our path. I look at Jan – his darling face, his wild hair, the red velvet beret crammed on his head; his battered boots, his paint-streaked jerkin. I try to imagine him surrounded by palm trees but my imagination fails me. There are too many oceans to cross.

Meanwhile he paints me: *Woman on a Bed*. I lie there, shivering in the cold. He paints fast, on a wooden panel. He gazes at me as if I am an object – that rapt impersonal gaze I remember from when he painted my portrait. When we speak, however, his face softens; he returns to himself. In his eyes I see one kind of love replaced by another.

Outside stretches the noisy city – bells ringing, horses neighing, carts rattling past. Here all is silent concentration. The water's reflection ripples on the walls; it dances like my dancing heart. I lie propped on his pillows, on the bed where I have found greater joy than I believed possible. My heart is full. I know that I will leave my husband and come to him; I've known this for weeks. In fact, I knew it the moment Jan stepped into my house.

He says: 'Whatever happens to us, this painting will not lie. It will tell the truth.'

≈§ 29 ?≈

THE PAINTING

To ornament a single piece most dearly
'Tis best by sundry means to improvise
Accessories that its deck'd gist revealeth
An artful play on art it doth comprise.

S. van Hoogstraeten, 1678

Nearby, in his house in the Jodenbreestraat, Rembrandt too is painting a naked woman lying on a bed. Curtains are pulled back to reveal Danaë, dressed only in bracelets, propped on a pile of pillows. She waits for Zeus to descend on her in a shower of golden rain.

The painting is drenched in gold – gold curtains, weeping golden cherub, the golden warmth of the woman's skin. But where is the rain, and can that approaching lover be truly a god? It looks more like an old servant.

She hangs in the Hermitage, the loveliest nude he has ever painted. But if not Danaë, who is she? She has been *Rachel awaiting Tobias*; in later years she became *Venus awaiting Mars*. She has been *Delilah awaiting Samson* and *Sara awaiting Abraham*.

At that time Rembrandt was deeply in love with his young wife, Saskia. Could this just be a woman, radiant with desire, waiting for her husband?

This same year, 1636, Salomon van Ruysdael paints *River Landscape with Ferry*. Livestock is being herded on to a ferry; the water is glassy, reflecting the sky. It is a painting free from mythology – it depicts no souls crossing the Styx, just cows crossing a river to get to better pasture on the other side. It tells no story but its own.

And meanwhile, in Haarlem, Pieter Claesz is painting a *Little Breakfast* – a herring on a pewter plate, a roll, some crumbs. It is a painting of transcendent beauty, with no lessons to be learnt. Art for art's sake.

Painters are simply artisans; they are suppliers of goods. Pictures on a grand theme – history or religious subjects – are sold for the highest prices. Next come landscapes and seascapes, priced according to their detail, then portraits and genre paintings – merry companies, interiors, tavern scenes. Finally, at the bottom of the scale are the still lifes.

Jan's painting, however, has no value. Its category is immaterial for it is not for sale. He works fast, with bold brushstrokes, for soon Sophia must leave and he wants to capture her, now, just as she is. Besides, she is chilly.

Centuries later she will hang in the Rijksmuseum. Scholars will quarrel about her identity. Is she Venus? Is she Delilah? Papers will be published about her place in van Loos's work. Ordinary people will wonder: who is she? His mistress? A model? Surely not a model, for she gazes out of the painting with such frank love.

She will have no title. She will just be known as *Woman on a Bed*. Because that is what she is.

❦ 30 ❧

CORNELIS

Thou hast begot children not only for thy selfe, but also for thy countrie, which should not only bee to thy selfe a joy and pleasure, but also profitable and commodius afterwardes unto the common wealth.

Bartholomew Batty, *The Christian Man's Closet*, 1581

Cornelis is down in his vault. The room is used for storage – wood, peat, old possessions. It is dark down here; he has lit an oil lamp. His whole house is now in shadow for summer has arrived and the linden tree outside is heavy with foliage. It is July; his wife is five months pregnant and her belly is starting to swell. Yesterday he asked if the baby was kicking yet. He stretched out his hand to touch her but she moved away. 'Not yet,' she said. 'It is not kicking yet.'

How can she understand his anxiety? She is young. God willing, she will never know what it is like to lose a child. She knows of his loss, of course, but the young cannot imagine the unimaginable; their blind confidence is a kind of solace. He needs to be reassured, however, that a living child lies beneath her gown, he needs kicking proof. For in the past God has offered him happiness, only to snatch it away.

Down in the vault Cornelis unlocks the chest. It is made of teak, imported from the East Indies, and veneered with copper; he hasn't touched it for years, it belongs to another life. He lifts the lid and gazes at the baby clothes. A scent of sweet woodruff is released; the herb, brittle as dust now, is strewn among the woollen robes. He lifts out tiny vests and jackets. He lifts out Pieter's velvet doublet and presses it to his nose. His son's smell has long since gone.

'*Here is your child*,' said the midwife, placing the baby in his arms. '*May our Lord grant you much happiness through him, else may He call him back to Him soon . . .*' The smell of spiced wine, the fragrance of his son's damp head. His wife eating a restorative meal of buttered bread and ewe's milk cheese.

How blessed he was. A son, an heir. What rejoicing was heard in his house that night. He offered up his prayers of thanksgiving, *We yield Thee hearty thanks, most merciful Father. . .* He kissed his wife. He put on the feathered cap of fatherhood, made of quilted satin. His whole country was enveloped with his gratitude. Was its birth not miraculous too – wrested from the ocean, blessed by God? Constantijn Huijgens, poet and humanist, Secretary to the Stadholder – a man whom Cornelis holds in the highest esteem – he says of their country: *The Lord's benevolence shines from every dune.*

In the corner of the room, dim in the shadows, stands the wheeled chair in which his sons learnt to walk – a wooden pyramid, on castors. It is dusty and now simply looks like a piece of apparatus. Within its cage he placed his sons and watched their legs working as they propelled themselves from room to room, stopping at the flights of steps. Cornelis thinks: once again I shall hear the noise of its castors, rattling over the floors.

He sorts out the baby clothes. This is woman's work,

but he wants to do it. He never thought he would open this chest again. Sophia is unaware of its existence. He will get Maria to wash and air the robes, and store them in the linen closet in readiness.

Cornelis, carrying the bundle, walks upstairs. He hears voices in the front room and goes in.

A strange sight greets him. Maria lies on the bench beneath the window. A gypsy woman bends over her.

Sophia swings round and stares at Cornelis. 'Dearest!' she says. 'I had no idea you were in the house.' She catches her breath. 'We met this woman in the market. She can predict whether it will be a boy or a girl.'

Meanwhile Maria has jumped up. She looks flushed. 'Sorry, sir.' She turns to Sophia. 'Go on, miss.'

Sophia settles herself on the bench, lying on her back. The gypsy woman dangles a string above her belly; a ring is tied to it.

'Clockwise it's a boy, the other way it's a girl,' Sophia tells him.

'Lie still,' says the gypsy.

A moment passes. The ring starts to rotate, gently. They watch it.

'It's a boy,' says the gypsy.

Sophia sits up. She stares, wide-eyed, at Maria. Why? Maria's hand is pressed to her mouth. Cornelis smiles benignly. They are just young girls, having fun. Sophia and her maid seem inseparable nowadays – always whispering behind closed doors. Pregnancy, he has noticed, causes women to close ranks. Still, he wishes that his wife could have a more suitable confidante, somebody of her own class.

Cornelis pays the old woman; she leaves.

It's a boy. Despite his suspicion of gypsies Cornelis wants to believe it. He turns to his wife but she has fled; he hears her slippers pattering upstairs. He had no idea that she was superstitious; pregnant women, he decides, can behave in a most peculiar manner. He doesn't remember dear Hendrijke acting like this.

Clutching the baby clothes, Cornelis smiles indulgently. It's a boy. He always knew this, in his heart.

'Do you remember, my dear, that I am travelling to Utrecht tomorrow, to visit my mother?'

'I will accompany you,' Cornelis replies.

'No.' Sophia lays her hand on his arm. 'I will only be gone for two nights, you have business to attend to. Isn't it tomorrow that you're expecting the shipment from England?'

'But in your condition –'

'It is an easy journey. Please, dear husband, this is a women's matter. My mother and I – we see each other so rarely – we have so much to talk about. And she is too frail for company. I would rather visit her alone.'

Cornelis understands this. However, he feels rebuffed that his wife's constitution can bear a fifty-mile round trip to Utrecht yet be unable to stand him lying with her in bed. She will not even allow him to gaze at her body. Her modesty in this matter makes him feel excluded. How he longs to touch her swollen breasts!

Sophia strokes his beard. She knows he likes this. 'I've prepared your favourite *hutspot*,' she murmurs. 'Can you smell it cooking?'

'Your sickness has gone?'

She nods. 'I feel much improved.' She does indeed

look well – flushed cheeks, bright eyes. 'Mutton, chicory, artichokes, prunes ... all your favourites, stewed with lemon juice and ginger ...'

He still feels hurt. 'Why do we never eat fish now-adays?' he asks petulantly. 'You know I like fish, but we have had none for weeks.'

'You told me you were tired of it, remember? You said that soon we would be sprouting fins.'

'It was just a joke.'

'Besides, I haven't wanted to cook it, the smell made me ill.'

She kisses him and leaves, the keys at her waist jangling. He hears her humming as she makes her way to the kitchen. What wayward creatures women are. Who would have thought that a visit to her mother would make her so skittish? Her moods switch so violently. Recently, when he suggested that they engage another servant, she had snapped at him.

'I can manage. Maria is quite enough.'

'This house is too large for one maid,' he had replied, reasonably.

'I don't want a man in the house, not in my condition. Let us wait until the baby is born.'

She is carrying his child, however. He loves her and he will humour her every whim. It is a beautiful evening. Cornelis fetches his pipe and gazette. He sits on the seat outside his front door. The sunshine, blazing between the leaves of the linden tree, dapples his house with light. His neighbour Mr Molenaer, sitting on his step, nods and smiles. Cornelis sits in peace, reading about the treacherous policies of Louis XIV. How corrupt is the French court, how venal the Spanish. Here, all is peaceful in the golden evening sun. Families have emerged to sit outside on their front steps. Children play at their parents' feet. Maria appears and empties a pail of slops into the canal. How bonny she looks nowadays, how fat and flourishing. In other countries servants are treated like slaves; here, in his enlightened city, they are considered one of the family. In the kitchen he can hear Sophia and Maria laughing like sisters. They have their girlish secrets – and why not, if it keeps them happy?

Cornelis's mind wanders. He thinks of Sophia's real sisters and the wretched circumstances in which they were living, five years before when he first visited their home. Their father, before he died, had been declared bankrupt. The bailiffs had removed the printing press and other assets from the house; the upper floors had been let to tenants. The girls and their mother were living in two rooms on the ground floor, eking out a living by taking in sewing.

A colleague of Cornelis, with whom he did business in Utrecht, had organized an introduction – for Cornelis was a rich widower looking for a wife and here were three girls of marriageable age. Sophia, the eldest, had served him spiced buns. How beautiful she was – shy and modest but not uneducated. After all, she had been brought up among books. She knew the old masters and that afternoon they had discussed the relative merits of Titian and Tintoretto.

What a world he could teach her! Sophia was clay, waiting to be moulded by his expert hands; she was fertile soil, waiting to be planted with the choicest of blooms. And she had responded to his advances. Demurely, at first, but there was no mistaking the warmth with which she had accepted his invitation of a trip in his carriage. Cornelis remembers that day down to the smallest detail for the past, even the near past, is more vivid to him than the present.

They had driven into the countryside. Sophia gripped the window-ledge. Entranced, she gazed at the fields, the grazing cows, the rows of willow trees as if she were a child seeing them for the first time. He thought: she is the daughter I never had. He gazed at the nape of her neck – the downy skin beneath her coiled-up hair – and longed to stroke it with his finger. Such a wave of desire he felt for her. *Fleshly conversation* – those were his words for sexual congress with his wife. A companionable, mutual comfort. This was different. This young girl – how desperately he wanted to protect her, but how he wanted to possess her, too! His heart was thrown into confusion.

The sky, the vast blue sky, was heaped with clouds. Below it lay a field covered with strips of bleaching linen. The strips of cloth, straight as rulers, stretched into the distance. The sun slid out from behind the clouds. The cloth, so blinding white; the cloud-shadows moving over it. Far away, figures toiled, unrolling another strip.

She pointed. 'Look at them. It's as if the earth is in pain and they're wrapping it in bandages to make it well again.'

Beneath his ribs his heart shifted. It was then that he truly fell in love.

The sun slips behind the houses opposite. Their stepped gables loom up, as jagged as teeth. Cornelis shivers and gets to his feet. He remembers the field of cloth. Now he thinks of the world as his child, as dear and as precious. The linen strips, they are swaddling bands, ready to wrap around his baby and hold it safe. His faith has been restored to him; God has finally heard his prayers.

This is a comforting thought. Why, then, does he feel so uneasy?

❦ 31 ❧

SOPHIA

Conduct thyself always with the same prudence as though thou went observed by ten eyes and pointed at by ten fingers.

Confucius

I want to hold you in my arms and feel you dreaming. His writing is branded in my heart. It is childish writing – Jan is an artisan, he has had little education, less than me, in fact. Words of love will for ever, for me, be clumsily formed.

We are going to spend a night together. Not just one night, two! – for such is my greed. My husband thinks that I am going to Utrecht. By now I have written to my family, telling them about my condition. They would have been eager to see me. I feel as guilty about betraying them as I do about Cornelis. At some point I must, indeed, visit them but I have been putting it off – they know me so intimately that they are bound to tell I am lying. My little sister Catharijn, in particular – she is sharp-eyed, she will guess there is something suspicious going on. I shall have to face them some time but not now, not yet.

Come to me and spend the night. I cannot believe it is really going to happen. When I slip into his studio during the day we cannot be alone – his pupil is there, sometimes his servant; once we were interrupted by a man coming to look at Jan's work and I had to hide behind the bed curtains. As for the evenings – even when my husband goes out it is riskier, now, to leave the house because it is high summer and the light lingers until nine. I have lost my ally, the darkness – that vast cloak that enveloped me more effectively than my own. Even when I succeed in getting there we only have an hour. At ten o'clock the nightwatch trumpet sounds and those who are out return to bed. What a blameless, hard-working nation we are. In bed by ten, faithful husbands and faithful wives. It is no city for lovers, for those out late on the streets are viewed with suspicion.

It is mid-morning. Cornelis is at work when I leave the house. He has given me some gifts for my family. I have hidden them in the attic. For some reason this seems as wicked as my larger deception.

I cross myself, praying for a safe voyage. No gale-tossed ocean holds more terrors than these sunny streets. No Spanish fleet, its guns trained in my direction, is as dangerous as my neighbours on their way to market.

Time expands and contracts. We hoard it like misers or watch it spill out like shaken cloth in front of us. Our dreams are broken by it – at night they are punctuated by the whirr of the nightwatchman's rattle and his singsong voice, jolting us awake to the hour. Then silence closes over us again. When I am alone in the house it seems endless – minutes crawl past.

In Jan's studio, however, I urge it to stay still. How can the sand fall so fast? But time spent there, when finished, has no end; it is with me always. And now time has a new momentum – nine months which quicken as they carry us helplessly towards November. From that moment it is unimaginable. In November, we step out of the building into space and this time I cannot imagine flying.

Just now, however, time feels motionless. Jan and I have spent the day in his bed. I have no idea of the hour; outside, the street noises seem miles away, in another country. He has sent Jacob home and given Gerrit the day off. He has stocked up with food for a siege of love.

On the floor, among my discarded clothes, lies my cushion. I am only five months pregnant; it is a small cushion, green velvet, that I have stolen from the library. Now that it is detached from my body it looks absurdly humdrum. I have grown fond of my fabric child, my plump accomplice.

I say: 'I will have to use a pillow soon.'

'What are we going to do, Sophia? We have to face it sooner or later.'

'Live for the moment,' I reply blithely. 'Isn't that what you said, when you were painting our portrait? Grasp it while you can.'

'But what's going to happen when the baby is born? Even if we run away he will find us.'

'Ssh – let us not talk about it now.'

'He'll track us down. There's nowhere we can go that is far enough.'

Jan is right. We have realized, upon reflection, that our plan will not work. Cornelis is a powerful man with influential connections. He knows the ships' captains; how can we travel undetected? Should we arrive at the East Indies, even then we would not be safe. Cornelis is in communication with traders there, he owns a spice plantation. Nowhere in the world will be safe.

'God will give us an answer,' I reply.

'You really think that He's on our side?'

'Where's your Bible? Get a key.'

Maria has told me about this. It is her transaction with God when she has to make a decision. Jan climbs into bed, carrying his Bible. It rests like a paving stone on our knees. I close my eyes, open a page at random and place his hand, holding the key, on some words.

'Read it out.'

He reads: *'Thy breasts are like two young roe deer that are twins, which feed among the lilies . . . Thy lips, o my spouse, drop as the honeycomb; honey and milk are under thy tongue.'* Jan closes the Bible. 'That's our answer.' He laughs, rolling on top of me. The Bible falls to the floor with a thud; the bed vibrates.

Before we sleep Jan sponges my face with warm water. I squat on his nightpot. As I do so he kneels beside me, unfixing my hair. These tender preparations make me weak with love. Every object here moves me, for he has touched it. Even the dusty floorboards, for they have borne the weight of him. The smell of linseed oil is more aromatic than all the spices of the East.

That night I sleep in his arms. *My beloved is white and ruddy; his cheeks are as a bed of spices, as sweet flowers, his lips like lilies dropping sweet-smelling myrrh.* I have never slept naked with a young man before. How sweet is his body, how sweet his breath! We sleep entwined. His skin is firm and smooth. He stirs and turns, cupping himself round my back, cupping my breasts in his hands. I am as tall as he is, we were made for each other. He presses his feet against mine, twin feet.

Far away, through my dreams, I hear the singsong: *Two of the clock! . . . Three of the clock!* My happiness is measured in hourly beats. Throughout the city citizens lie together, husbands and wives, in their wall cupboards. In the drawers beneath them lie their children, lawfully begotten. Families sleep, snug in their furniture. I have left all that behind; I have pulled out to sea . . . tonight I am adrift and there is no returning to my former life.

Jan breathes into my hair. He exhales his dreams; they seep into me like sea mist. Shamefully I think: if only Cornelis would die. My lover and I could sleep together every night, for the rest of our lives.

This is such a monstrous thought that I put it from my mind. Instead I dream of how it would have been if I had met Jan first and were free to marry him, to love him blamelessly. It was nobody's fault that I married Cornelis – oh, there was pressure from my mother, but I could have resisted her. I have only myself to blame for what was, I now see, a sacrifice of my youth and my hopes. I did it to save my family from ruin, but what terrible ruination awaits us all now, if I cannot think of a way to extricate myself and Jan from this reckless plan we have set in motion?

If only Cornelis were dead.

Suddenly I sit up, wide awake. Jan stirs; he runs his tongue down my backbone.

'I have thought of a plan,' I say.

'What plan?' he murmurs dozily.

'There is only one way we can escape. And for him never to think to look for us.'

It is an idea so obvious, so breath-takingly simple, that I am amazed I didn't think of it before.

*

If this plan is to succeed we need money, a large amount of money. Quite how much, we need to find out. We need some now, to put it into action. Then we will need a great deal more money in November, when the baby is born.

We are sitting on the bed; sunlight streams over the half-shutters. A bird sings outside the window; a child shouts. We have lost track of time. We have eaten nothing. I still feel winded, as if I have been hit with a sackful of sand.

'Remember what my husband said, about the madness that has gripped our country?'

'You are the madness, sweetheart.' He strokes my wrist. 'You are the one who's gripped me.'

For once I don't respond. 'This tulipomania.'

Of course he knows of it. Everyone has been infected, it has spread like fever; in the past year it has grown out of control. Secret deals are struck in taverns, huge fortunes have been made. Our staid burghers have become men possessed.

'One bulb – remember what he said? One bulb sold for all those goods – horses, silver . . .'

'What are you suggesting?'

'One bulb sold for the price of a *house* – I heard last week – the freehold of a house on the Prinsengracht . . .'

I am damp with sweat. We sit there, wedged together on the bed. I am wearing his nightshirt. On my lap a red drop appears. For a moment I think it falls from the ceiling. Another drop appears, and then another. I have a nosebleed. This happens when I am agitated.

Jan presses a handkerchief to my nostrils and holds back my head. Between his fingers the handkerchief reddens. Nosebleeds are strange because you bleed without pain. The handkerchief grows sodden. When Jan releases my head he has blood on his hands.

THE TULIP GROWER

Select a large bulb with several well-developed offsets. Clean off the soil from the offsets and pull them away from the parent bulb, taking care to preserve any roots. Prepare pots with a moist, sandy compost. Inset a single offset into each pot, and cover it with compost. Label, and water.

Royal Horticultural Society, *Encyclopedia of Gardening*

Claes van Hooghelande is a man possessed. In his house on the Sarphatistraat he sleeps fitfully. He is a tulip grower. He used to be a tax collector but now he has given that up, much to his wife's dismay, so that he can stay home and watch his garden. It is only a small garden, but it is the centre of his universe. Beneath the soil, out there in the night, his babies are fattening.

His real children lie sleeping upstairs but he has no time for them any more; they have been forbidden to enter the garden, on pain of a beating, and have to play in the street. When he thinks of them, which is seldom, he pictures them as nodes on a tulip bulb – offsets nestling against the parent bulge. Everything he sees speaks tulip to him. Comely women are tulips; their skirts are petals, swinging around the pollen-dusted stigmas of their legs. The taxes he used to collect are precious nodes prized from the plump bulb of a yearly wage.

He is obsessed with nodes. The more nodes, the heavier the bulb. The heavier the bulb, the more *azen* it weighs. The more *azen* it weighs, the more money for him. That is why he leaves his tulips in the soil for longer than his rivals, the other amateur growers whose gardens are now empty earth. They lifted theirs in June, but he has waited weeks longer.

It takes its toll on his nerves, however. Despite his precautions – his trip wires, his round-the-clock vigils – while his bulbs are still in the earth they are at risk. Thieves, dogs, slugs. He used to be a corpulent man with a healthy appetite; in pre-tulip days he could hardly squeeze through his front door. Now he cannot eat; he scarcely sleeps. His clothes hang loosely on him; his wife has had to take them in. He suffers from heartburn and has to drink tinctures of peppermint and brandy. He and his wife used to sleep in a bed downstairs, built into the back-room wall. With the money he made, last season, he bought a free-standing bed and has moved it upstairs next to the window. From here he can see down into the garden.

Compost is his secret. All autumn he prepared the soil, digging in his magic mixture – cartloads of cow dung, sackloads of chicken excreta, fine sand, and bonemeal from the slaughterhouse. Since then he has applied thrice-weekly applications of his special fertilizer. He has worked out the ratio per foot and written it in a book, which he keeps locked in his strongbox.

'You'd dig in your children if you thought it would improve the soil,' mutters his wife. She doesn't understand. Sometimes she looks at him strangely. He likes to squat in the garden, crumbling the earth between his fingers, sniffing it. No sweetmeats smell more delicious; he could gladly eat it.

'Maybe, my love, you should see a doctor,' says his wife. Wait until she sees the prices he will get. Sixty thousand florins in four months, that is the profit one man has made, the other side of the city. That is sixty times his annual income. See her face then. *And this man has a smaller garden.*

Claes has already lifted and stored most of his bulbs, his Miracles, his Emeralds and his main stock-in-trade, his Goudas. He has triumphed this year, perfecting several new varieties – his own home-bred mutations which he is yet to name. One of them bears an indigo blush like a drop of ink dissolving in milk. He has split off their nodes, weighed them and packed them in straw. These he has stored in his vault, under lock and key, to wait until the prices rise. His Admirals – Admiral van Enckhuysen and Admiral van Eyck – still lie under the soil. Last night he dug his hand into the earth and cradled a bulb with his fingers, feeling how it had fattened up. He felt the thrill of a deviant, rummaging under a man's nightshirt to fondle his balls. When sailors were caught doing this they were sewn into sacks and thrown into the sea. What punishment awaited those who fondled an Admiral?

Maybe you should see a doctor. Why? He is simply a man in love. How beautiful they were in bloom – blousy and seductive, moving gently in the wind. How vast were their flowers, nourished by his secret tonic (soot and his own urine). They were his choicest of children. They were his company of angels, trumpeting soundlessly. How he loved them, the intensity varying according to their value. The financial scale is this: first the yellow-on-reds (Goudas); then purple-on-whites; and finally the most thrilling of them all – the red-on-whites.

Semper Augustus is a name he can only whisper, as if in church. The kings of kings, the holiest of holies. He has five of them slumbering under the soil. He grew them from five offsets he purchased the year before – five was all the investment he could afford. Five flowers have bloomed – petals as white as a virgin's brow, veins as ruby-red as blood, their chalices blushing as blue as a summer sky. Solomon himself could not sing of them with greater fervour. *Behold, thou art fair, my beloved, yea, pleasant; also our bed is green.* They are his five dazzling maidens. *Thy lips are like a thread of scarlet . . . Thou art all fair, my love; there is no spot in thee . . . Thou hast ravished my heart.*

They have died down now; beige tatters are all that remain. Their beauty lies beneath the soil, to which we shall all return. Tomorrow is the big day. Tomorrow he shall lift them . . . they will rise like Christ from their long sleep; their resurrection shall make him rich.

Claes sleeps. He dreams of the soil breaking open. Soldiers rise from it, their spears bright. He turns, bumping against his wife, and sinks back into slumber. He dreams of an intruder. It's a large black dog. Stealthily, it lopes through the streets . . . lightly it vaults over the wall . . . soundlessly it lands in the garden. It looks around, baring its white teeth in a grin. It leaps into the tulip bed and starts digging. It digs up tiny arms and tiny legs, the dismembered limbs of Claes's children.

The bell jangles. Claes sits up, wide awake. He leaps out of bed. Flinging open the window, he yells: 'Who's there?' Down in the garden more bells are ringing. He sees something move – a blacker clot in the moonlight.

And now he is out in the garden, tripping over his own trip-wires, setting off the bells again. They peal dementedly, calling the sinners to be punished.

Claes examines the earth. In the moonlight he sees a footprint. Nothing has been disturbed. This particular sinner has got away. The alarm system has been Claes's salvation.

❧ 33 ❧

SOPHIA

All these fools want is tulip bulbs.

Petrus Hondius, *Of de Moufe-Schans*, 1621

There is a knock at the door. Gerrit, Jan's servant, stands there holding a letter.

'What has happened?' I have a sinking feeling of foreboding. 'Has something befallen him?'

'No, madam.' Gerrit is a phlegmatic man – stolid, with a face as lumpy as putty. He comes from the swamps of the Marken where the peasants move sluggishly in perpetual fog. Nothing that has been happening arouses his curiosity, for which I am grateful.

I tip him. He leaves and I tear open the letter. Jan has had cold feet. He is not going to go through with it.

Destroy this when you have read it. I'm wrong. Jan tells me about his attempted robbery last night. See? Another crime has been added to the list. But he was interrupted, he says. The man woke up. Luckily Jan escaped without being seen. *We will have to buy the bulbs.*

This is a small set-back, but we will manage. I will have to raise some money to help pay for them. We will have to buy a considerable number of bulbs, to spread our speculation and cover our inevitable losses. Upstairs I open my jewellery chest. Pearl ear-rings, my pearl necklace, sapphire bracelet and pendant. There isn't a great deal of it. Though generous to my family, and to myself in many ways, Cornelis is parsimonious when it comes to jewellery. Precious stones do not interest him. He prefers to spend his money on paintings, on embellishments for his home and on our own fine clothes. His in particular. He is surprisingly self-indulgent in this respect. When I arrived at this house I counted in amazement the items crammed into his linen cupboard: thirty pairs of drawers, seventy shirts, twenty-five collars, forty pairs of ruffled cuffs, thirty ruffs, ninety handkerchiefs . . . The closet is burdened to breaking-point; last week we had to call in a blacksmith to repair the hinges.

I pick out some items of jewellery and lay them on the bed. I cannot pawn it all – Cornelis will notice – but I can spirit these out of the house.

Maria comes in. She knows about our plan, of course. She has to, since it revolves around her. She agreed to it, but she still seems in a state of shock.

I tell her about the failed theft. She gazes at the few pieces of jewellery laid out on the coverlet. They look pitiful, like small slaughtered birds after a poor day's shooting.

'I'm frightened,' she says.

Maria cannot talk like this. She is the sensible one, the practical one. I pretend not to understand. 'We will get enough money, don't worry,' I tell her. 'We'll get the bulbs and then we will make a lot more.'

'I'm not frightened of that.'

It is night. I step into the courtyard. The flowers breathe courage on me. I invest them with courage, knowing that their blowsy lives are soon over. Despite their beauty, they are insensible. Little do they know that we recognize, through their brief blossoming, the futility of human endeavour.

I pause, breathing in their scent. There is a purity about our love of flowers; it is an act of homage untempered by greed. Tulips are the exception to this; when I think of them lust rises within me, a shameful wave of heat. I think: next year I shall plant tulips in this narrow bed. Then I realize that there will be no next year.

I pace around the yard like a condemned prisoner. In the darkness I feel a crunch under my foot. When I was being prepared for marriage I was told the proverb of the snail: she is a good housewife, carrying her home with her wherever she goes.

Well, this particular snail is gone; and her house with her.

JAN

PIETER   *I like you very much. That is why I want to propose to you this advantageous transaction. I do it without any self-interest, and out of pure friendship.*

HANS   *I am listening carefully, my friend.*

PIETER   *I have a bulb of the tulip 'Harlequin'. It is a very beautiful variety, and in addition much sought after on the market.*

HANS   *But I never had anything to do with flowers in my whole life. I don't even have a garden.*

PIETER   *You don't understand a thing. Please listen to me; don't interrupt because who knows, maybe today a great fortune is knocking at your door. Can I go on?*

HANS   *Yes, yes, of course.*

PIETER   *Well, the 'Harlequin' bulb is worth a hundred florins, and maybe even more. In the name of our unblemished (as I said) friendship, I will let you have it for fifty florins. Still today, without any effort, you can make quite a lot of money.*

HANS   *This is indeed a splendid proposition. Nothing like this has ever happened to me before. Only tell me, please, what am I to do with this 'Harlequin'? After all, I will not stand at the street corner . . .*

PIETER   *I will tell you the whole secret. But note it down well in your memory. Why are you fidgeting?*

HANS   *I am listening, only I'm a bit dizzy.*

PIETER   *Do exactly as I say. Go to the inn At the Lion. Ask the innkeeper where the tulip vendors meet. You will enter the room he indicates. Then someone will say in a very thick voice (but don't you be put off by it): 'A stranger has come in.' In answer to that, cluck like a chicken. From that moment on you will be included in the community of vendors.*

Contemporary play, quoted in Z. Herbert,
Still Life with a Bridle

A week has passed and Jan, in his studio, is trying to make a deal with the man he attempted to rob. It is unnerving to stand there with him in broad daylight, but there is no way the man can recognize him. He is the only grower Jan has heard of – his name was given to him by a drinker in the Cockerel tavern, who said that Claes van Hooghelande had a substantial hoard, rigorously guarded. Jan is only too aware of this, now.

The tulip grower fidgets. He looks restless, as if he is longing to get back to his house. He has told Jan that all his bulbs are now lifted and stored under lock and key. There is a manic gleam in his eye.

'I have five Semper Augustuses,' he says, his voice hoarse with excitement. 'A little out of your league.'

The trouble is, the bulbs he has brought along are also out of Jan's league. Jan has the money from Sophia's pawned jewellery, his own savings and a loan from Mattheus, but there is still a shortfall. At this stage he needs to buy heavily. He has ordered a bagful of Goudas – red-and-yellow, the cheapest of the flames – plus several thousand *azen* of some Admirals whose full names he didn't catch. *I've wasted my time collecting taxes*, joked Claes, *I've joined the navy now*. Only if Jan buys heavily now will he make the fortune which is, literally, a matter of life and death.

'Take a painting.' He grabs Claes's arm and leads him to the canvases. 'Take a *Raising of Lazarus*. That's worth thirty florins.'

He pulls out canvases and panels, and leans them against the wall. Jacob, who is grinding pigment, stares.

'Take a *Sacrifice of Abraham*, take a *Landscape with cows*.'

'But, sir –' says Jacob.

'Be quiet!' barks Jan. 'Take a *Woman taken in Adultery*.'

Claes van Hooghelande stands there, scratching his head. 'What about that still life over there? Those flowers?' He points to a panel, propped in the corner. 'Look – see there – between the columbine and the guelder-rose – see that tulip? That's a General of Generals.'

'It is?'

'You painters, you're such ignoramuses.'

'We just paint what we see.'

'Oh yes?' replies Claes. 'Daffodils and lilies, blooming together? That's impossible.'

'Not impossible when *I* paint them.' Now it is Jan who fidgets.

'Such a graceful tulip, such a poem of blooms,' says Claes. 'You have caught it to perfection – the drop of dew –'

'Thank you, but –'

'Strange, isn't it? That flowers are transient but a painting lasts for ever.' Claes's voice throbs with emotion. 'Yet one bulb of that tulip is three times more precious, in financial terms, than your painting of it. Try to sort that one out.' Recovering himself, he speaks briskly. 'Throw in that painting and you have a deal.'

Jacob gasps. Jan ignores him.

Just bags of onions, that is what they look like. For them, Jan has paid as much as he makes, with luck, in a year's work. How homely they look. Yet they are more valuable than jewels, than paintings, than gold. Stored within those bulbs, fattened by sunshine and rain, is his future.

Jan feels too restless to work. He longs to speak to Sophia. He misses her desperately; she is so near yet so far, locked into her echoing prison. He wants to tell her about Claes, the manic gleam in his eye and those loose breeches that he kept hitching up. He longs to tell her everything in his head, those words he stores up for her until they meet again. Is she thinking of him now? What is she doing – sewing, gazing out of the window, the sun shining on that beautiful bumpy nose? He longs for her so much that he feels winded. He tells himself: just a few months and we will be together, for ever.

He walks past her house but there is no sign of life, no face at the window. Maybe she is shopping. He walks down to the market-place but it is late, the stall holders are packing up. It has been such a strange day that he has lost track of time.

Coachmen lounge beside their horses, waiting for fares. When a customer arrives they throw a dice to decide who will take him. Jan thinks: how stolid we look, but underneath we are all gamblers. We are a people possessed. And mine is the biggest gamble of all.

That night he dreams that people are tulips, stem necks

rising from their ruffs. Their heads nod; they bend this way and that in harmonious agreement. It seems entirely natural that Amsterdam is peopled with blooms.

He is in the town square, calling out to Sophia. She walks towards him, nodding. It must be Sophia; he recognizes the violet dress. He asks her to accompany him across the seas. She nods more vigorously. Her petals fall, revealing a naked stalk.

Jan's friend Mattheus knows a crooked doctor. His name is Doctor Sorgh. He performed an abortion on a maid that Mattheus had impregnated and was paid with a painting of *Peasants Carousing*.

'Why do you want him?' Mettheus leers. 'Got some tart in the family way? When will you stop fucking around and settle down with a nice girl, eh? Gerrit makes a terrible wife. Wrong shape, for a start.'

Jan meets the doctor in an apothecary's shop down by the docks. This turns out to be a mistake. Doctors hate apothecaries because they steal their custom. They belong to the same guild and pass themselves off as physicians, sitting under their stuffed crocodiles and giving muttered consultations. They even wear the same outfits – black robe and coat, pointed hat.

'Why did you want to meet me here?' snaps Doctor Sorgh.

Jan thought it seemed appropriate. The doctor flounces out and they sit down in a nearby tavern.

'So what is it?' asks the doctor.

'You did my friend a service some years ago. Both parties were satisfied and he recommended you as some-one of discretion.'

Doctor Sorgh has a narrow, foxy face and ginger hair. Jan needs to trust him. This man holds three lives in his hand – four, counting the baby. By now Jan feels a certain protectiveness towards Maria who is the most vulnerable of them all. He feels almost as responsible as if he has impregnated the girl himself.

'I want you to deliver a woman of a child. The woman's safety is of the utmost importance –'

'You think I'm incompetent?'

'No!' How touchy this man is! 'No – but there are some unusual circumstances about the case. Secrecy, for a start.' Jan pauses. He has to take this man into his confidence; he has to tell him the whole story, otherwise their plan won't work. He swallows a mouthful of beer and begins. Telling a stranger like this, hearing his own voice telling it, unsettles Jan. The whole enterprise sounds insane.

There is a silence. Doctor Sorgh gazes into his beer. Jan looks at the physician's hands: long, white fingers. They stroke the side of the tankard. Jan tries not to think where those fingers have been.

'The risks,' says the doctor at last. 'The risks are enormous.'

'We have to take them. You see that, don't you?'

'Risks to the maidservant, risks to your friend.' Doctor Sorgh looks at him. 'You must love this woman very deeply.'

Jan nods.

Unexpectedly, the physician sighs. 'You are a lucky man.'

There is a silence. The doctor strokes the tankard with his slender, fastidious fingers. It is early afternoon. The tavern is empty except for three young sailors – comely young men who sit at a table playing cards.

Doctor Sorgh looks at them. 'I once loved someone,' he says. 'But cowardice . . . I succumbed to cowardice. I could not face the world's condemnation . . . losing my livelihood . . . Too much was at stake. I've regretted it all my life.' He lifts the tankard; his hand is trembling, however, and he puts it down. 'To be courageous . . .'

His voice trails off. Jan gazes at the floor. On it lies a broken pipe stem and an empty oyster shell. They resemble the prints in a book of emblems. Jan thinks: if this were a painting I would understand what he is trying to tell me.

'That's why I try to help people out,' says the doctor. 'All life is a risk – I'm a physician, I'm only too well aware of that. But some people sail closer to the wind and they are the ones after my own heart. I admire them for that, you see, because I have been incapable of doing it myself.'

Jan is moved by this. He is starting to like this prickly, emotional man. Then he looks at Sorgh's trembling hands and wonders: is he fit for this?

Maybe the doctor senses this. He says: 'She will be in safe hands.'

'Which she?'

'Both of them.' He rallies. 'Now, the question of money.'

He tells Jan his terms. A sum in advance for himself and the services of a midwife – he will supply a midwife, a woman he trusts implicitly.

Jan counts out the money. He does this with a careless shrug. It is only money; it is just a few bulbs. Underneath his insouciance, however, he is profoundly excited. Tulipomania has claimed him too and what a mistress she is! She flirts with other men, she leads them on. In the end, however, just when he thinks he might lose her she surrenders to him. She gives herself up gladly to his arms and a spasm of pleasure floods his body. For a while he is sated. Then the hunger rises again; the hunger is unslakable. That is the sort of mistress she is. Who could resist her?

A month ago, back in July, he was an innocent, a virgin. Speculators were *kappisten*; he thought they were mad. Now he has joined them and already he has tripled his investment. His Admirals led him into battle and what booty he brought home. For their price has rocketed and now he has enough to pay this doctor today and invest in new bulbs. He hardly has time to paint. Each day he returns to the taverns where his new friends, the equally smitten, buy and sell in a feverish fog of tobacco smoke.

'And then I need your bond for the final settlement,' says the physician.

He tells Jan the amount. Jan's jaw drops.

'You must consider the risks,' says Sorgh. 'To me.'

Just for a moment, thinks Jan, I thought this man was sentimental. He gets out a piece of paper. *I, Jan van Loos, do promise thee* . . . He writes down the sum in his big, clumsy writing. So many noughts! He draws the 'O's with professional pride; they are perfectly round. His master trained in Rome, where Renaissance instruction taught him such things. They are as round as a full moon in a *Seascape at Night*. They are as round as bubbles blown by a child in a painting by Hals, to tell us of the futility and brevity of life.

Doctor Sorgh folds up the note and puts it into his pocket. Jan shakes his hand. All life is a gamble. After all, it is a gamble that he was born at all. His parents' love-making, the night before or the night after, would have produced another child. It is a gamble that he met Sophia, the love of his life.

He will get the money. He knows how to gamble with mistress fortune, he has learnt the game. And when it comes to the final, biggest gamble of all, he knows that he will win. For luck, so far, has been on his side.

❧ 35 ❧

AUTUMN

While the dogs yelp, the hare flies to the wood.

Jacob Cats, *Moral Emblems*, 1632

Autumn gales sweep across the land. Rain lashes the countryside. Trees are uprooted; rivers burst their dykes and flood the fields. Great stretches lie under water, returned to the element from which they emerged. Boats sink and their wreckage is tossed contemptuously on to the beaches, as if God were throwing away empty walnut shells. Cornelis's ships return, but the largest vessel in the Archangel-Muscovy convoy, laden with a cargo of sable, ambergris, whale train oil and iron, goes down without trace. Church bells toll for the souls of the drowned.

In Amsterdam chimney-pots topple into the street and washing is lifted from lines. A builder is blown off the scaffolding of a half-built mansion in the Keisergracht, a martyr to the hubris of wealth. Walking beside the canals is treacherous; people overbalance in the wind. Bodies are found floating in the water, casualties of drunken despair, for tulipomania has ruined many and they drown their sorrows for the final time.

Then, in mid-October, the rain stops. Fog blankets the city. Noise is muffled, the buildings invisible. People cannot tell where the streets end and the water begins. They stumble into the canals and drift undiscovered for days, until the fog lifts.

Nights are eerily still. Fog rises off the water. Figures can slip through the alleys undetected for the fog is so dense that a man can scarcely see his hand in front of his face. Amsterdam is a city of ghosts, of crimes that leave no trace, for those who commit them are swallowed up into the vaporous night.

ᴥ§ 36 §ᴥ

SOPHIA

A fool and his money are soon parted.
Proverb on tulipomania in Visscher's *Sinnepoppen*, 1614

I offer up a prayer of thanks. This fog is God's smoky breath, guarding us. I can slip through the streets unseen. Spectres loom up, pass and are gone; they keep their heads down, watching their step. We are all muffled in cocoons.

Jan and I have grown bolder. My bedchamber faces the street. Cornelis, in the other room, is a heavy sleeper. At night Jan throws a pebble at my window and I creep down to let him in. I cannot risk taking him into my bed. Besides, love-making nowadays is not the first thing on our minds. We are inflamed by a new lust and huddle on the settle, whispering.

I have written down the sums. Jan takes the piece of paper; it shakes in his hand. Time and again we have gambled and won. Jan has joined the big league now. He is trading in the white, on tulip futures. He and I speak like experts. We have long ago lost sight of bulbs; they have become an abstraction. We are buying bulbs we have never seen and for which we have not yet paid, gambling on new varieties, that their price will rocket, trading onwards and upwards. Bulbs have been bought and sold ten times in one day without anyone laying eyes on them. We hunch over the paper and examine our sums, those dazzling pencil marks. I am so excited that I have another nosebleed and splash them with my blood.

It is not just love-making that has been forgotten. Jan has long since stopped painting. Consumed by his fever, he spends the days in four different taverns, whispering the password to enter the rooms where the trading takes place. I cannot go with him and risk being seen; the whole town seems to be in the taverns now. He bids Through the Plates. Wooden discs are circulated. Unit values are written on them in chalk. The men haggle; bids are added and wiped off, and the deal celebrated with a glass of wine. Jan takes out loans from his friends to finance the next deal and repays them double their money within the week. It's magic! God is smiling on us; He is on our side.

I rub my blood off the paper, leaving a brownish smear.

Over the past weeks Maria has changed. She has grown big, of course, fattening up like a bulb nourished by the finest compost. The other night, at dinner, Cornelis remarked: 'Have you seen the size of her? She's eating us out of house and home.'

'She has always had a hearty appetite,' I replied.

She moves differently, too, swaying like a ship in full sail. Exertion makes her breathless. For months I have been performing her heavier duties, cleaning the house and washing the floors. She mustn't lose this baby. Exertion makes *me* breathless too. I have never worked so hard in my life. Our reversal of roles – me into servant and she into mistress, restricting herself to the lightest tasks – extends beyond housework.

'Funny, isn't it?' she says one day. 'You dressed up as me and I used to dress up as you.' She tells me that she would clothe herself in my blue jacket, the one trimmed with fur, and parade in front of the mirror. We have even exchanged hands. Mine have become maid's hands, cracked and dry. 'Rub them with goosefat.' She chuckles. 'Then you will be a lady.' Hers are as soft as a gentlewoman's.

The house has changed, too. I have become familiar with it now – back-achingly familiar: the Delft tiles along the skirting, each playful child; the marble floors that seem to stretch for miles. Upstairs I polish and repolish the wide floorboards. Sleeves rolled up, I scrub and wipe, and rise to my feet groaningly. The embossed walls of the Leather Room catch the dust; pain jabs my shoulders as I stand on a chair, wielding my broom. Down in the kitchen I rub the brick floor with a sodden cloth. Before, the house consisted of rooms in whose chairs I sat, whose floors I crossed and whose windows I opened when I gazed into the street. It was the painted background to my life. Now I am intimate with every chipped brick, every knot of wood. If only we could employ another servant. But that, of course, is impossible. We cannot risk a stranger among us during this crucial time and I have resisted my husband's attempts to hire one.

I am now in my final month and wear a bulky pillow strapped around my waist. Mrs Molenaer, my next-door neighbour, has lent me several of her maternity gowns. Maria has simply sewn extra panels into her dresses. Bending down is difficult – how do pregnant women do it? I am tempted to pull out the pillow, but what happens if Cornelis returns unexpectedly? He has become increasingly solicitous, popping in during a working day to check that I have not suddenly gone into labour.

Doctor Sorgh has visited. Upstairs he examined Maria and pronounced her in fine health. He washed his hands, came downstairs and told Cornelis I was as fit as a fiddle. He has a narrow face, like a greyhound; I have never trusted a man with ginger hair. I must admit, however, that he played the charade to perfection. When he left he whispered: 'Your friend is right. You are a bold and singular woman.' Maria told me that his hands smelt of violets.

Maria has changed in another way. Over the past weeks she has retreated into herself. She sits alone in front of a dead fire. She sits for hours at the front window, remaining there until the light fades, as if waiting for a visitor who never arrives. Worse than this, she has grown apart from me; our old sisterliness has vanished.

'You and your sums!' she says one day. 'All you think about is money. What about *me*?'

'I'm doing this for you! You will benefit as much as me. Soon it will be over and we'll both be free.'

'It's easy for you,' she snaps. 'You've changed, Sophia.'

She calls me *Sophia* now, not *miss* or *madam*. I do not mind. I know her anger is caused by fear. She is facing childbirth; she is about to embark on a voyage through the most perilous waters – a voyage she must take alone, for nobody can accompany her.

Yesterday Jan made sixty-five florins profit. *Sixty-five florins*. The blacksmith who mended our linen cupboard pays that for a year's rent; he grumbled about it.

'Gamble on tulips,' I said. 'It's easy.'

'Pride comes before a fall,' he replied. 'Mark my words, they're fools, the lot of them.' He was a miserable old soak.

I meet Jan in our trysting-place beside the water fountain. He has lost weight, his cheeks are sunken. His hair, so shiny and curly when he first came to my house, is matted. He doesn't greet me; eyes glittering, he grabs my wrist.

'Tell me we should do it! Do you have the nerve?' His grip tightens. 'Luck's been on our side, all these weeks. Tell me we should put all our eggs into one basket!'

He means, of course, the risk beyond all risks: the most dangerous risk of all. The king of kings, the Semper Augustus. Claes van Hooghelande has one bulb left.

It will take all our money, every stuiver, and a great deal more. More huge loans. The price has been fluctuating wildly. It is all or nothing. But if we succeed we can wipe out all our debts, when the baby is born, and be set up for our new life.

'I think we should do it,' I say.

'My darling, my petal,' he replies.

We sit there in silence, stunned by our decision. *My petal* is what Jan calls me, nowadays.

The baby is due any day. As luck would have it, Maria's belly is small – a neat bulge carried low. To a casual observer she is simply a large girl, bulky under her layers of winter clothing. She seldom goes out now, and when we do walk to the market eyes are focused on me, a ship in full sail. Pregnant women soak up attention. Besides, Maria is a servant and even in our enlightened country servants are on the periphery of our vision.

When we are alone together, however, we can relax. Though this is hardly the word to describe our state of heightened tension. Maria's womb has assumed enormous importance to us; its magnetism is more powerful than the moon pulling the tides. The old light-hearted days have long gone (Maria giggling to me: 'Wouldn't it be comical if *you* fell pregnant too!'). Now we have entered the last phase; we are in deadly earnest.

My bedchamber has been prepared in readiness for the birth. Our neighbours have rallied round. A wooden linen warmer has been installed behind the fire-screen. Our neighbour Mrs Molenaer has lent us her wickerwork cradle, shaped like a boat. My husband has laid out the birthing robe in readiness. On the shelf sits a gruel cup and spoon, to help me through the labour, and a bowl for spiced wine to drink after the happy event. Another neighbour, who has a groom, has offered his services to fetch my mother when the labour pains begin, but I have told him that she is too frail to undertake the journey. In fact, I have lied to my family about the delivery date; they expect the baby to be born several weeks hence.

The real delivery, of course, will not take place in this room. When Cornelis is at work I take Maria up to the attic. She huffs and puffs on the narrow stairs – they are scarcely more than a ladder – and stops half-way to catch her breath.

It is a small, dark room, its ceiling criss-crossed with heavy black beams. Cornelis has not come up here for years; nobody comes up here. I have cleaned the room, swept away the cobwebs and strewn lavender on the floor. I have made up a birthing couch; it is a simple bed that must have been used by a servant long ago.

In the corner leans my picture, *The Love Letter*. There is my painted self, alone with her dreams, poised at her own moment of decision. She looks so virginal, so untried. That decision has long been taken; I can hardly recognize that maidenly creature now.

Maria sits down on the bed, groaning. Her back aches. I sit down next to her and rub it.

'He's a good doctor,' I tell her. 'And she is a highly experienced midwife. Over a thousand successful deliveries, she says. You will be in safe hands.'

Suddenly Maria bursts into tears. 'I want my Willem,' she wails.

'They will look after you, my darling.'

'I want him with me.'

'He's not coming back.'

'I want my Willem!' She's sobbing uncontrollably now. Her face streams with tears and snot. 'How could he leave me, *now?*'

'He doesn't even know. You've got to forget him.' I wipe her nose with my handkerchief. 'Soon you will have a lovely baby –'

'I want him!'

I try to cradle her in my arms. This is difficult, with two great bulges blocking the way. Unable to reach her I stroke her instead – her hair, her belly.

Beneath her apron I feel movement. The baby is kicking. He kicks with such force that my hand jolts. He is pushing against me fiercely.

'Feel him,' I say. 'He's trying to get out. And when that happens, he will set us all free.'

JACOB

I am sending you a human figure for your studies to become a painter ... Use this figure, don't allow it to stand idle as it was here but draw assiduously, especially those large, animated human groups for which Pieter Molijn liked your work so much. If you paint, paint contemporary things, scenes from life, they can be done the most quickly. Be tenacious so you complete the paintings you have started; you will be loved for them, with God's help, just as you were loved in Haarlem and Amsterdam ... Serve God above all, be modest and polite towards every man, in this way you will assure your success. I am enclosing also clothes, long brushes, paper, chalk, and all the beautiful paints ...

Letter to Gerard Ter Borch from his father, 1635

Jacob is an ambitious young man. He knows that he is going to go far. Though he is only sixteen he has his life mapped out. By the age of twenty-five he plans to be an established painter, with his own studio. He will specialize in portraits, for here in Amsterdam there is an unlimited supply of potential clients who wish to see themselves immortalized on canvas. By the age of thirty he will have made his name with a major commission – a militia painting, a guild group, a Civic Guard banquet. Not only is one paid by the individual portrait – head-and-shoulders so much, full-length more – but the picture then hangs in a public place and ensures that one's fame spreads abroad.

His role model is not Jan, about whom he has mixed feelings. Those he admires are Nicolaes Eliasz and Thomas de Keyser, successful portraitists at the height of their fame. They are commissioned, paint to a reliable standard and deliver their canvases on time. After all, painting is a trade, like any other; those who succeed are those who give good value for money. His other idol is Gerrit Dou, a past pupil of Rembrandt van Rijn. How different is Dou from his erratic and temperamental master! Dou's fine detailing means that his paintings are in high demand. The collector Johan de Bye owns twenty-seven of them; the Swedish ambassador in The Hague pays a thousand florins a year – *a thousand* – simply for the promise of first refusal. Dou's is the style to which Jacob aspires. Neatness and order, not the baffling self-indulgence of Rembrandt or the florid brushwork of the Antwerp phenomenon, Peter Paul Rubens. Jacob likes to be in control.

Painting is a job, not a gamble. Jacob distrusts excess. This tulip craze that has enslaved his countrymen leaves him cold. He feels nothing for it but contempt. Unlike his master, he is not a dreamer. The only indulgence he allows himself is a Saturday stroll through Amsterdam's most prestigious residential streets where the new mansions are being erected; as he passes, he speculates on which house he will buy when he makes his fortune. When the time is right – when he has established himself – he will find a suitable girl from a good family and settle down. But not yet. Not now.

In several respects Jan van Loos has been a disappointment to him. For a start, he keeps a disorderly studio. When Jacob arrived it was a pigsty. The brushes looked as if they had been chewed by rats. When customers arrived Jan greeted them in his bespattered old painting clothes – were they not due some respect? Then there is that ramshackle servant wandering in at all hours – where does the man sleep? The gutter?

Worse than that, Jan is clearly dissolute – Mattheus was right to warn Jacob about this. Jan has plainly been fornicating with that married woman. When Jacob returns home each night he does not confide this to his parents. They would be horrified and take him away.

It is this sexual excess, no doubt, that has caused Jan to neglect his work. Loss of spermatozoa enfeebles a man and thins his blood. Then there is this tulip business. Nowadays, Jan is looking even more disreputable – wild eyes, ragged beard. The man has not had a haircut for months. Where is his professionalism? Some days he doesn't go near his easel at all.

Of course, this is a disappointment. Jacob was expecting more instruction. But it has also worked to Jacob's advantage. He had expected his first year to be taken up with mundane tasks – binding brushes, lacing canvases on to stretchers, sharpening metalpoints and preparing the white ground on the panels. If he were lucky, he would get to copy some of the master's works.

Nowadays, however, Jan is often out. Even when he is in the studio he is distracted. He is late in fulfilling his commissions and has started relying on Jacob to help him. In the past few months, in fact, Jacob has become more his master's partner than his pupil. During the summer Jan began three paintings to sell on the open market – a *Landscape with Shepherds*, a *Rape of Europa* and a canvas depicting – most appropriately, in Jacob's opinion – *The Effects of Intemperance*. He has also embarked on a portrait commissioned by a prominent official in the Stadholder's court. But he never has time to paint them and has told Jacob to complete the canvases. Not just backgrounds, not just clothing – the entire painting.

Jacob is only too delighted to do this. He knows that his talent is equal to that of his master. This, combined with his single-minded industry, will make him ultimately the more successful of the two. Sometimes Jacob considers that it is *he* who should be giving lessons to his master.

And then comes the bolt from the blue. It is the first week of November. Jan has been offered an important commission: a group portrait depicting the Regents of the Leper Hospital. And he has turned it down.

'Why?' asks Jacob, his brush poised.

'Because I have to go away.'

'I beg your pardon?'

Jan pauses. 'I must apologize, Jacob. I have been meaning to tell you.' He sits down heavily on the bed. 'Things have been – well, in a state of some confusion recently. I have to go overseas.'

'When?'

'In two weeks. On urgent business.'

'When are you returning?'

Jan shakes his head. 'I am not returning. I shall be gone for good.' He looks up at Jacob as if seeing him for the first time. 'I'm so sorry.'

Trembling with anger, Jacob lays down his brush. 'You cannot do this, sir. You contracted to teach me for two years –'

'If you knew the circumstances –'

'You gave your word!'

'– maybe you would understand –'

'My parents pay you fifty florins a year –'

'I will reimburse them –'

'What about my examination? What about my membership of the guild –'

'I will find you another master. Mattheus can take you, I'm sure he will find room for you – I'll insist –'

'You – you –' Jacob splutters for a word. He is not used to swearing. 'You *wretch*!'

Jan gets up and puts his hand on his arm. 'Jacob, believe me. It is a matter of great importance.'

'To *you*,' Jacob spits, shaking off his hand. Just then there is a knock at the door. Jan answers it.

A boy steps into the room. For a moment Jacob thinks: it is all a lie. Jan is getting rid of me so that he can take on another pupil. I am too talented – that is the answer – he's jealous that I will show him up.

Jacob is wrong. The boy passes Jan an envelope.

Jan opens it and looks at the contents. Then he goes to his strongbox and scrabbles among his papers. He brings out a purse of money and gives it to the boy. 'This is the deposit. Tell him I will make up the full amount on the day – it's all right, it is all agreed.' He scribbles something on a piece of paper. 'Here is my bond.'

Later, Jan goes out. He never bothers to lock his strongbox; he is the most careless of men.

Jacob opens the box and takes out the envelope. He opens it. Inside lie two tickets of passage on the *Empress of the East*, sailing on the fifteenth of November to Batavia, East Indies.

❧ 38 ❧

MARIA

Though the bird's in the net, it may get away yet.

Jacob Cats, *Moral Emblems*, 1632

The baby is overdue. He was due in the first week of November and already it is the twelfth. Maria is pulled two ways. She wants him to hurry up and be born; she wants to get it over with. She even feels a sense of obligation to the others – the sooner she performs her part of the bargain, the sooner they can leave. Sophia told her that their passage is booked for the fifteenth of the month. Time is running out. If this baby is not born by then they will have to cancel it and book a later date, but that might be weeks or even months hence. Maria is still enough of a servant to feel this obligation.

On the other hand, she is terrified. *It's like being torn apart*, said her butter-churning grandmother. *It's like all your guts they're being pulled out.* Thump-thump went her pole. *It's like being slit open with a red-hot knife.*

Maria misses her grandmother; she misses her mamma. Now that her time is near she aches for them even more strongly than for Willem. Who is going to take care of her? Not her mistress, that's for sure. She will be occupied elsewhere. Maria feels utterly alone.

That night she sleeps fitfully. The baby is kicking. Her belly is a rock; she cannot turn over in bed. She prays to the baby: don't be born tomorrow, not on the unlucky

164

thirteenth. Please wait until the next day.

She dreams her dream again. How painlessly her babies slip out, shoals of them . . . She floats through the submerged rooms, swimming in her underwater palace, her babies flicking behind her.

The next morning she is chopping the heads off sprats when the pains begin.

39

SOPHIA

As you sow, so shall you reap.

Jacob Cats, *Moral Emblems*, 1632

I hear a cry and I hurry into the kitchen.

Maria is doubled up. 'It's started,' she mutters.

I help her up to the attic room – one flight of stairs, then another, then another. It seems to take for ever. At the top Maria has another contraction and has to sit down.

I have laid a fire in the little room. I light it and settle Maria on the bed.

'I want my mamma,' wails Maria. 'Don't go.'

'I'll be back in a minute.'

'Don't go!'

I hurtle down the stairs and out of the house.

⋙ 40 ⋘

MRS MOLENAER

Fear is a great inventor.

Jacob Cats, *Moral Emblems*, 1632

Mrs Molenaer sits in her parlour. She is singing a ditty to her baby Ludolf as she wipes his bottom.

> *Sleep, little child, sleep,*
> *Outdoors is walking a sheep*
> *A sheep with white feet,*
> *That's drinking the milk so sweet . . .*

Baby Ludolf gazes up at her with fathomless under-standing. How lucky she is. Each day, before she rises, Mrs Molenaer offers up a prayer of thanks. She lives in a handsome house in the Herengracht. Her husband is a kindly man who loves his family. As Chief Inspector of Hygiene he holds a prominent position in society. He gives generously to the poor and has a fine baritone voice. In the evenings he sits in his cap and dressing-gown, surrounded by his children, and says *There is no greater happiness on earth than this*. He plays draughts for hours, patiently, with his eldest son.

Mrs Molenaer is roused from her reverie by a battering at the door. Her maid ushers in Sophia, her heavily-pregnant next-door neighbour.

'The baby's started,' gasps Sophia, clutching her belly.

'Please could you get a message to my husband, down at his warehouse?' She stops, doubled over in pain. She breathes heavily for a moment and then straightens up. 'And could you send the de Jonghs' groom to this address?' She shoves a piece of paper into Mrs Molenaer's hand. 'It is where the midwife lives. Tell him it's urgent.'

Mrs Molenaer rises to her feet. 'My dear, I will come to the house with you –'

'No! My maid will attend on me until the midwife arrives.'

Sophia hurries out. Mrs Molenaer frowns. Why on earth didn't the maid deliver the message herself? Fancy letting her mistress do it, in her state. What a fat, lazy slattern that Maria is! Mrs Molenaer has always thought so. Whenever she has seen her lately the girl seems to be sitting down, taking a break from her none-too-onerous duties. She has grown huge with sloth. And she's pert, too.

Mrs Molenaer washes Ludolf's bottom with a damp cloth. Her maidservant would not behave like that. But then she has always been blessed with excellent servants. It is just another aspect of her great good fortune.

❧ 41 ❧

CORNELIS

How you stare at this flower, which seems to you so fair,
Yet it is already fading in the sun's mighty glare.
Take heed, the one eternal bloom is the word of God.
What does the rest of the world amount to? Nothing.

Jan Brueghel the Elder

Cornelis paces up and down. Cries of pain float down from Sophia's bedchamber. Each cry pierces his heart. If he could but bear the baby for her. He would give up everything – his house, his wealth – to ease her agony.

On the table sits the sandglass. He has already turned it twice; she has been in labour for two hours. He paces back and forth across the floor. The marble squares measure out the intervals between her cries . . . black . . . white . . . black . . . white . . . like some grotesque game of chess. *We are but playthings of God.*

The room seems unnaturally still, as if it is holding its breath. Outside, it is overcast; daylight barely filters through the window. On the shiny oak table, with its bulbous legs, sit the sandglass, an uneaten apple and a pair of polished candlesticks. They look like the stillest of still lifes. *Natures mortes*, the French call them – a phrase that has always unsettled him.

A yell comes from upstairs – hoarse, indescribable, an inhuman noise that drains his blood. On the wall hangs *Susannah and the Elders*. Her plump flesh taunts Cornelis.

He used to find it arousing – how disgusting that seems now, for look where his brutish desires have led him: to inflict this suffering on the woman he loves best in the world. How obediently Sophia submitted to his lust, night after night, and what is the result? This horror, where he cannot follow her.

Oh most powerful and glorious God, we Thy creatures, but miserable sinners, do in this our hour of distress cry unto Thee for help . . . save her, oh Lord . . .

Black . . . white . . . black . . . white . . . now there are fewer steps between her cries. The contractions are coming faster.

Look down, we beseech Thee, and hear us calling out of the depth of our pain . . . hear me, oh Lord my God . . .

Black . . . white . . .

For we adore Thine divine majesty and implore Thy goodness . . . help, Lord, and save us for Thy mercy's sake . . .

The midwife hurries downstairs and into the room. 'Please send for Doctor Sorgh,' she says.

'What has happened?'

'There is no cause for alarm. I simply need some assistance.'

The midwife tells him the doctor's address. Where is that damn maid? Cornelis grabs his cloak; he will have to go himself. How could Maria disappear when she is most needed? Upon his arrival home, when he rushed in to see Sophia, she told him that Maria had popped out on an errand to the tailor's, but that was hours ago. The tailor's shop is only a few streets away. Where in God's name is she?

Cornelis rushes out to get the doctor himself. It has started to rain.

❦ 42 ❧

JAN

Grasp all, lose all.

Jacob Cats, *Moral Emblems*, 1632

In a fug of tobacco smoke Jan paces up and down his studio. Outside it is raining. Noon . . . He has turned the sandglass three times since the urchin brought Sophia's note. Maria has been in labour for three hours.

Jan feels helpless – a mere man, when two women are in danger. For weeks, absorbed by his own business, he has hardly given Maria a thought. Now he feels for her with every bone in his body. He fears for them both; Sophia is taking her own terrible gamble. What a woman she is. What women they are! He is impotent. He can do nothing except smoke pipe after pipe of tobacco. In sympathy, his stomach is gripped by cramps. He urges Maria to give birth to a healthy child, for its delivery will be his deliverance.

Oh Lord, if in Thy wisdom Thou spare this woman, I will mend my ways and serve Thee in righteousness all the days of my life . . .

He needs God now. How blithely he has broken one Commandment after another: *Thou shalt not covet thy neighbour's wife . . . Thou shalt not commit adultery . . .* How he laughed at Sophia's religious scruples. Once they leave Holland he will become a changed man. He might even convert to Catholicism.

He pictures Batavia. He has more information about the place now. Gone are its pagan palm trees and sensual self-indulgence; that was simply a day-dream. Batavia, he has learned, is altogether more sensible. Built on the ruins of ransacked Jacatra, the town is growing into a little Amsterdam: gabled dwellings, canals, bridges, a court-house and churches. There are even mills to pull energy out of the suffocating heat.

Jan makes a bargain with God. If in His goodness He spares them and they survive the journey, he and Sophia will live like model citizens. They will be pillars of this new colony and go to church twice every Sunday. He promises God this, with all his heart.

⋅⊰ 43 ⊱⋅

CORNELIS

Mankind's hopes are fragile glass and life is therefore also short.

Anon.

Cornelis lets the doctor into the house. They are both soaking wet. Doctor Sorgh makes for the stairs. When Cornelis tries to accompany him he puts his hand on his arm. 'Remain here, sir,' he commands.

'But I –'

'It is no place for a husband. If you want to be of use, fetch us some more hot water.' He hurries upstairs.

'Maria!' shouts Cornelis. There is no reply. Where *is* the girl?

A scream issues from the bedchamber. Cornelis's blood freezes. If only he could comfort his wife. He knows that it is no place for a husband, but it tears at his heart.

In the kitchen he pumps water into the pot. His hands are trembling. He must trust this doctor but why, oh why, did Sophia insist on his services rather than those of Doctor Brusch? There is something odd about Doctor Sorgh – that lisping voice, those fluttering gestures. And the man has red hair, always a sign of doubtful integrity.

Cornelis puts the water pot on the stove and stokes up the fire. He seldom comes into the kitchen; this domain belongs to Sophia and her maid. Cornelis gazes at her copper pans hanging on the wall. Inside the glass-fronted treasury he glimpses trenchers and sauce-boats, familiar to him from a thousand companionable meals. How neat is her little kingdom where, aided by her maidservant, she prepares his food with wifely devotion! On the table is a covered dish. He lifts the lid. Headless sprats lie there. They look pitiful – bodies one side, heads in a pile. The triangle heads stare at him with their glazed, baleful eyes.

❦ 44 ❧

JAN

Put a curb on thy desires if thou wouldst not fall into some disorder.

Aristotle

Darkness has fallen. Rain lashes at the window. It has been seven hours now and still no word. Jan does not expect a message for some time yet, but he can almost feel the people in this city who wait, poised to go into action. Maria's labour has lit a touch-paper.

Seven hours! How time drags, but labours can take double this time. Triple. His mother told him that he took two days to struggle into this world and in doing so nearly killed her. He longs to go to the house in the Herengracht, to see if everything is going according to plan. Without seeing for himself he can scarcely believe that it is happening. His earlier anxiety has been replaced by a sense of unreality.

His studio, too, looks unfamiliar. He has packed up in readiness to leave. His paintings, wrapped in sacking, are stacked along the wall ready to be delivered to Hendrick Uylenburgh, the dealer, who will sell them and forward the money. Jan is only keeping his drawing books and his paintings of Sophia. They are packed into his trunk, ready for the voyage. Also in the trunk are his own clothes and two of Sophia's dresses, smuggled out of the house.

In two days he and Sophia will be gone. Maria's timing is perfect. Tomorrow he will discharge his debts; on the fifteenth, at dawn, they will set sail. It has all been successful so far – all but the final gamble upon which it hinges.

Jan cuts a slice of cheese, splits open a roll and eats. He is alone. Jacob left a week earlier, still rigid with fury, slamming the door behind him. Nowadays Gerrit only pops in occasionally. He has been phlegmatic about Jan's departure. He has always helped out at the local tavern heaving barrels, and he is now in his bumbling way working there full-time. Jan is fond of his servant who has been loyal to him, in his manner. When he gets his hands on the money, before he sails, he will pay Gerrit off handsomely.

Lightning flashes. Jan jumps. Thunder crackles, with a sound like tearing cloth. Above him, the heavens are splitting open.

45

CORNELIS

The end makes all equal.

Jacob Cats, *Moral Emblems*, 1632

It is late at night. Outside, the storm rages. Cornelis sits hunched beside the fire, drinking brandy. The cries upstairs ceased some minutes ago. Now there is a deathly silence.

He cannot move. He has been told to wait here. Although he has put on his dressing-gown he is still shivering. It is cold outside and the fire gives off little heat in this great room. He wants to suffer, however, in his own small way.

Then he hears a cry upstairs. Faint, but unmistakable.

He hears the cry again – a thin wail, like a kitten. Joy floods through him. He drops to his knees and clasps his hands together. *Oh my Lord, I offer up my heartfelt thanks for Thou hast heeded my prayers . . .*

He stops. Footsteps are descending the stairs.

The midwife comes into the room. She is a massive, square woman, built like a barn door. In her arms she carries a bundle. Cornelis rises to his feet.

'Sir,' she says. 'You are delivered of a fine baby girl.'

The bundle stirs. He sees black, damp hair. He is about to speak when something stops him. It is something in the midwife's big, perspiring face.

177

'I offer my condolences, sir,' she says. 'We could not save your wife.'

Upstairs Doctor Sorgh restrains him at the doorway. 'Just for a moment – you may just see her for a moment. Please don't touch her. There is a danger of contagion spreading.'

'Contagion?'

The doctor pauses. 'I have reason to suspect that your wife was suffering from an infectious fever.'

'The plague?' Cornelis looks at him stupidly. He must be still sleeping. He urges himself to wake up.

Cornelis puts his hands on the doctor's shoulders and moves him aside like a chair. He steps into the bed-chamber. It is stifling hot. A bitter smell fills his nostrils, and something sickly, like violets.

Sophia's face is covered with a sheet. The doctor pulls it down, just for a moment. Sophia's face is revealed. It is pale, peaceful, and bedewed with sweat.

'We did all we could,' says Doctor Sorgh. 'She is at peace now, with the Lord.'

Cornelis bends towards his wife's face. The physician grabs his arm and pulls him back.

'Let me kiss her!'

'No, sir.' The doctor's grip hurts his arm. 'You must arrange for this room to be fumigated and for the bedding to be burnt. Necessary precautions, I am afraid . . . the fluids, the blood . . .'

The room looks strangely blind. The doctor has turned the pictures to face the wall. It is the usual custom, but now it seems like a bizarre game. Cornelis gazes numbly at his wife. It is all a game. She is just pretending. In a moment she will open her eyes and sit up. *It is all over, my dearest. Look! We have a beautiful daughter.*

The doctor ushers him out of the room. The corrupt, sweet smell clogs Cornelis's nostrils. He looks at his wife for the last time, her long humped shape under the sheet. Being drawn up over her head, it has exposed her feet. They look ludicrously naked. If he waits, she will wriggle her toes. She does not care to sleep like this; she likes to curl up, her knees under her chin.

The doctor shuts the door and accompanies him downstairs. Cornelis thinks: I cannot leave her there, she is so alone.

They sit down beside the fire. The physician is speaking but Cornelis cannot reply; his throat has closed. *It cannot be true.*

'I blame the foul waters of our city,' says the doctor. 'Do you know how many deaths by fever have occurred this autumn?'

Cornelis does not know. He does not care.

'Had she shown any signs of sickness?'

Cornelis tries to think, but the process is too laborious. He wishes this man would stop talking.

'Had she recently been complaining of headaches?'

His wife has been snuffed out like a candle.

'Sir?'

'This last week – yes,' replies Cornelis. 'She has twice taken to her bed with a headache.'

'The fever attacks the brain. Did she demonstrate any other unusual behaviour?'

Cornelis remains silent. Sophia has, of course, been acting oddly. Not wanting to be touched. Jumpy if he even approached her.

'One of the symptoms is tender skin,' says the doctor. 'Burning, as if it is on fire.'

'You have been looking after her, all these months,' blurts out Cornelis. 'Why didn't you tell me there was a danger?'

'Your agitation is understandable, sir, but I did not suspect she would succumb to this particular contagion. I simply found, in my first examination, that she was of a frail and vulnerable constitution. Any excitation might have triggered an inflammation of the womb, which would then spread through the blood to the brain.' He coughs. 'That was why I suggested . . . er, marital abstinence.'

He pauses. Cornelis looks at the doctor's white fingers. Why could they not have saved her?

'The body –'

'How dare you call her that!'

'I'm sorry. Your wife – she cannot stay here. I will arrange for her remains to be removed from the house immediately, to await burial.' Doctor Sorgh laces his fingers together. 'This is a terrible loss for you, I know. But you will be glad to know that your baby daughter is not affected. She is in fine health.'

Cornelis sits, numb. Around him swirl currents of activity. He hears muffled voices upstairs; doors opening and closing. Heavy footsteps descend the stairs; strange men are removing his wife. Something bumps against the wall. Cornelis cannot bear to look up. What right have they to do that? She does not belong to them.

A cup of hot gruel has been placed in his hand. He has a sense that Mrs Molenaer is here fussing over him, fussing with the baby. It is the middle of the night, but the neighbouring women are rallying round. He is sure they are being kind but he hasn't the energy to thank them, nor even see who they are.

None of this is happening. He cannot take it in, it is still a dream. Sophia is playing a joke on him, as she joked with her sisters. She is too alive to die. Her sewing frame lies on her chair, where she left it; her foot warmer sits on the floor waiting for her long narrow foot to place itself on it again. When he opens his eyes she will be sitting there, lifting her face to smile at him before she bends down again to her work. The light is dim; she raises the sewing frame closer to her face. She shifts in her seat, with a little sigh, to rest the other foot on the warmer.

God cannot play this cruel trick on him yet again. What sort of God is this, who would do it? . . . Cornelis is on the beach . . . he is a boy again. His father presses a shell to his ear. A roaring fills his head – a roaring from far away. '*It is the breath of God*,' says his father. '*Everything in your heart, He can hear it.*'

Outside, the roar has subsided. The storm is over. Cornelis seems to be lying in his bed, in the Leather Room. He gazes at the window. Dawn has broken; grey light filters through the thick panes of glass. He can now feel Sophia's absence in the house – a hollowness, a stillness, simply the lack of her. His wife has been washed away like driftwood; how quietly, how un-complainingly she has slipped in and out of his life. His years with her seem like a dream, dreamt up by an old man who has gazed into paintings and known that, even if those people ever stood there, poised in a room, they have long since gone. They are but shadows ... the gleam of a dress, burgundy red in the candle-light, the tilt of a head, the proffered glass of wine that has long since been drunk. That was never drunk in the first place. They have gone, and even his pictures are turned to the wall.

He thinks: art remains in the present tense, long after we humans are consigned to dust. He feels this has some significance, but he is too fatigued to work out the meaning.

He must have been dozing. The doctor, before he went, gave him a draught of something chalky and bitter. Grief has not hit Cornelis yet; it waits in the shadows like a footpad.

Maria comes in. He has forgotten about Maria. She looks unsteady on her feet; for a moment he thinks she is drunk. Staggering into the room as if she is in pain, she supports herself by holding on to a chair.

She says: 'This is a terrible loss, sir.' She looks all disordered – grey, damp face; matted hair.

He vaguely remembers that she should have been here – where was she? – but his brain is fuddled. Besides, he has no energy to rebuke her now.

'Oh, sir, what can I say?'

'My poor girl.' She is not drunk; he realizes this now. She is just overcome with grief. 'I can see this has devastated you, too.'

She sits down heavily in the chair. 'Oh, sir,' she says.

'You look quite undone.'

She nods, wordlessly, and gazes into the crib. There is a tiny, mewling sound, a sound in miniature. He has forgotten about the baby. Maria leans over – she stops half-way, grimacing in pain – then she lifts out the moving bundle.

'What has happened tonight, sir, is very terrible. It is God's will that your wife was taken, but it is also His will that He has given you a daughter.' She holds the baby in her arms and strokes the damp, dark hair. 'A beautiful, healthy daughter and for that we must be thankful.' She kisses the baby, breathing in her scent. 'I will care for her as if she was my own child.'

Cornelis starts crying – deep, wracking sobs. He has no energy to hide this from her. When Maria sees him her own eyes brim with tears. She moves beside him and places his daughter in his arms.

AFTER THE STORM

They are generally not so long-lived, as in better airs, and begin to decay early, both men and women, especially at Amsterdam . . . Plagues are not so frequent, at least not in a degree to be taken notice of, for all suppress the talk of them as much as they can, and no distinction is made in the registry of the dead, nor much in the care and attendance of the sick; whether from a belief of predestination, or else a preference for trade which is the life of the country before that of particular men.

William Temple, *Observations upon the Netherlands*, 1672

After the storm the city lies becalmed. It is a sunny morning, still and cold. Branches litter the streets like broken limbs. People clear away the wreckage. They swarm around like ants whose anthill has been scuffed; how doggedly they rebuild their lives. The Dutch are a hard-working, resourceful people; when their land is flooded they pump out the water and drain it again. They are used to repairing the ravages caused by the wrath of God, for He has sent these tempests to test them.

Along the Herengracht the sun shines on the great gabled houses. It warms their new red brickwork and the stone scroll-work around their doors; it blazes on the leaded glass of their many windows. How impressive they are. Monuments to the wealth and good fortune of

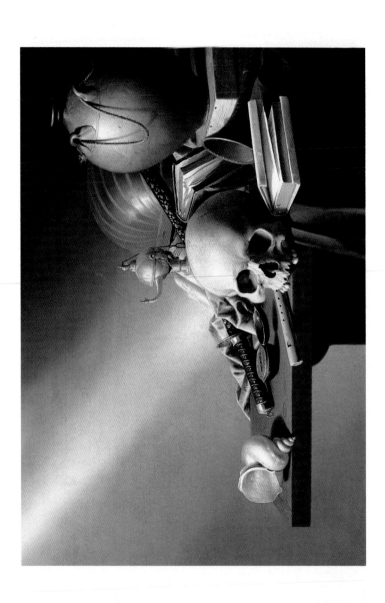

those who live within them, for this is the noblest street in the city.

The opposite side of the street, however, is plunged in shadow. There is a hush about it; the blind windows reveal no sign of life. In Cornelis Sandvoort's house the shutters are closed. During the night a death occurred; he lost his young wife in childbirth. He is a widower for the second time. Neighbours pause outside, shaking their heads. How cruel, for it to happen to him again when he should surely expect his wife to outlive him, providing him with comfort in his declining years. And some say that she was suffering from a pestilence too. Just a rumour, but the body has been removed for the safety of her surviving family. There will be no days of mourning around an open casket.

Mr Sandvoort must be sleeping; he was up all night. The neighbours do not yet disturb him, to offer their condolences. But if they listen carefully they can hear, through the shutters, the faint mewl of a baby. One life has been taken, to bring another into the world.

⊰ 47 ⊱

JAN

He that sendeth a message by the hand of a fool cutteth off the feet and drinketh damage.

Proverbs XXVI

Jan is woken by a knock at the door. The sun is shining; it is midday. After his tumultuous night he fell asleep at dawn and slept like the dead.

Gerrit stands there. He looks awkward – his hands hanging, his big meaty face blushing. 'Just come to say goodbye, sir, and to express my best wishes for the future.'

'Ah! You've come for your money.'

Gerrit shuffles his feet.

'Let me get dressed,' says Jan, 'and I will go and fetch it for you.'

'I'll come back later –'

There is another knock at the door. Gerrit opens it while Jan pulls on his breeches. Doctor Sorgh comes in. He looks exhausted – grey skin, bruised shadows around his eyes.

Jan gives him a chair. 'I received the message.'

Sorgh nods. 'It all went according to plan. A straightforward delivery, thank the Lord, she is a healthy young woman.'

Jan is still groggy. For a mad moment he thinks the doctor means Sophia. Then he realizes. 'I'm most grateful to you,' he says, buttoning up his shirt.

186

'I have come to collect the balance.' The doctor indicates the servant. 'Can we talk freely?'

Jan shakes his head. His bladder is bursting. He wishes the doctor would come back later, when he can think clearly. It is hard to think of payment for something he can scarcely believe has happened.

He says to Gerrit: 'Go into the kitchen and fetch some wine for Doctor Sorgh.'

Gerrit leaves. Doctor Sorgh says: 'You have the bill for my services and those of the midwife. There is a small extra charge for the – shall we say pallbearers? They were not included in the original agreement.' He passes him a piece of paper. 'But it adds little to the final amount.'

'Come back this afternoon, at your pleasure, and I will settle up with you then.'

Jan explains the situation. How, a month earlier, he bought the Semper Augustus bulb for a large sum. The grower, Mr van Hooghelande, has been guarding the bulb for him under the tightest security.

'You know what's happened to its value these past few days?' Jan's voice rises in excitement. 'The price doubled, then slumped, and now, if I can believe the information I've been given – and there's no reason to doubt it, my source is impeccable – when trading closed last night the price had reached four times the sum I paid for it, and today it rose again!'

The physician, however, shows little interest. He sits there, making a steeple with his long white fingers.

'So I will go there now and collect the bulb,' says Jan. 'There's several consortia waiting to bid for it, down at the Cockerel, and by the end of the day you'll have the money in your hand.'

There is another knock at the door. Gerrit returns, ushering in a boy. For a moment Jan fails to recognize him.

The boy says: 'I've come to collect the money for your tickets.'

'What tickets?' asks Jan stupidly.

'Two passages to Batavia,' says the boy, 'on the *Empress of the East*.'

'But I arranged to pay on the day –'

'My master says because you're sailing at dawn it has to be the day before.'

'You're leaving the country?' The doctor's voice is sharp.

'And he's not coming back,' adds Gerrit.

'All right, all right! I'm going to get it.' Jan turns to the physician. 'Come back this evening at six. It will all be sorted out then.'

There is a silence. Doctor Sorgh looks at him, at the packed-up room, at the other small creditor waiting restlessly. 'I would prefer to wait here,' he says 'if you don't mind.'

Jan stares at him. 'What?'

'No disrespect, sir. But in my particular line of work . . . maybe you can understand . . . the type of people I do business with . . . Well, one has to take some elementary precautions.'

'You think I'm going to slip my leash?' Jan is dumbfounded. 'Is that it? You think I'm going to run away?'

The doctor shrugs. 'I would prefer not to put it quite like that –'

'You don't trust me?'

There is a silence. The three of them look at Jan. The doctor says: 'Please do not take it personally. I would just be happier if you and I stay here together and you send your servant.'

Jan gets to his feet. 'Why don't you accompany me?' He goes to the door. 'If you don't want to let me out of your sight, come with me. We'll all walk there together.'

The boy replies: 'I've got orders to stay here with you. Not to leave your house until I have the money in my hand. That's my orders, sir.'

It is a stalemate. Jan looks from one face to the other. Doctor Sorgh examines his sleeve. The boy fidgets with his cap, turning it round in his hand as if he is primping pastry.

'Send your servant,' repeats Doctor Sorgh. 'Then we can get this whole . . . matter . . . over and done with.'

Jan sits down heavily on the bed. Gerrit, with his stupid, trusting face, raises his eyebrows. He is unsure, exactly, what is happening, but he is upset to see his master in a state of distress.

It is not an ideal situation. Jan trusts Gerrit with his life, but does he trust him with this? Gerrit is waiting; they are all waiting.

Jan takes him into the kitchen. 'Gerrit, you heard what the fellow said. I want you to run some errands for me. As fast as you can. No loitering, understand? Just think of it as your final errand, for old times' sake.'

Gerrit nods. 'W-w-what do you want me to do?' He has always stuttered, as if his tongue is too big for his mouth.

It is vitally important that Gerrit does not understand the value of the package he will collect from Claes van

Hooghelande's house. Jan has a nightmare vision of Gerrit's reaction – even trustworthy, faithful Gerrit – if he knew that in his hand he held the price of a house in the Prinsengracht. It would test a saint. Even if Gerrit doesn't run away with it he might be tempted to brag. Jan pictures him bumping into one of his drinking companions, pointing to the package and saying, *Never guess what I got in here*. Even if Gerrit doesn't steal it, there's a real danger that someone else will. Gerrit keeps even lower company than Jan.

Jan must think up some more errands to disguise the importance of this one. He presses some money into Gerrit's hand. 'Get me some pigments – here, I will make a list. And get me half a dozen cinnamon tarts, from the pastry shop, for these gentlemen here. And get me a package. It is waiting for me at this address.' He writes it down on a piece of paper; his hand is shaking. 'It is in the Sarphatistraat, on the other side of the city. Can you manage that?'

Gerrit nods.

'And come straight back here, is that understood?'

'Yes, sir.' Gerrit turns to go. Jan pats him on the back, as if he is a father sending his son out into the big world for the first time.

Jan stands at the window. He watches Gerrit lumbering off down the street. At least he is going in the right direction.

Jan thinks: this man has my life in his hands.

❧ 48 ❧

CORNELIS

The old man . . .
Although his limbs all grow stiff, his heart is quick,
He knows that no one will stay here, which is why
He fixes his limits and pays close attention
To the path and Word of God, towards the Gate of Life.

D. P. Pers, 1648

Cornelis is writing the death announcement. *It has pleased the eternal and immutable wisdom of Almighty God to call to His bosom from this sinful world to the blessed joy of His eternal kingdom, on the thirteenth day of this month, at the eleventh hour of the night, my beloved wife Sophia, after the noble lady had been confined to her bed in childbirth –*

He stops. He realizes, quite suddenly, that he has lost his faith. The words are just marks on a piece of paper; pious scratchings, as meaningless as an invoice for a bale of cotton. More meaningless. In fact, entirely devoid of any sense whatsoever.

God does not exist. Cornelis's small resurgence of faith has been extinguished. For thrice-twenty years he has paid his dues – in tears, guilt and fear – and what has he got in exchange? What is his return on his investment? Two dead wives and two dead children. What sort of a bargain is that?

All his life predicants have thundered at him from their pulpits. *God will punish you! God will seek you out, oh*

sinner! Prepare yourself for the flames of eternal damnation!
Once, when he was a little boy, he had wet his breeches.
They rail against the theatre, against tobacco smoking,
against coffee drinking, against excursions to the
countryside on the Sabbath, against festivities, against
pleasure, against life.

Who were they, these miserable men with their lank
hair and screeching voices? Who were *they* to tell him
anything? What did *they* know? Why did they presume
that *they* were the saved, these narrow-minded bigots
who saw sin in the smallest child and whose only joy was
to kill the joy of others? What God would appoint *them* as
his mouthpiece? If they wanted to rant, why not rant
against a God who allowed a lovely young woman to die,
in agonies, while giving birth to Cornelis's child?

Cornelis sits at his desk. He replaces his pen in its
stand. He thinks: has it really pleased the eternal and
immutable wisdom of Almighty God to call Sophia to His
bosom? What sort of a bosom is that? And she is not a
noble lady. She was his darling sweetheart. How pompous
he has been in the past. He remembers her polite face as
she listened to his pronouncements. Such pontifications.
How could he have presumed to know anything when he
knows nothing at all?

It is a strange, airy feeling; not unpleasant. Cornelis
feels as light as a husk. One puff of wind and he will float
up from his chair. Perhaps this is shock. Maybe his grief
at her death has made him temporarily insane.

He feels more sane, however, than he has ever felt in
his life. In recent years his doubts have troubled him.
Now Sophia's death has set him free. Far from
deepening his faith it has removed his belief altogether

and he feels like thistledown – up, up he floats to join her. Except she is not there in heaven, of course, because it does not exist.

Downstairs, down in the real world, he hears Maria singing to the baby. How lucky he is to have her. Maria is untroubled by theological doubt; she has the robust good sense of those who pay lip-service to God and then get on with their lives. Her earthiness is deeply reassuring. She couldn't care less that he has lost his belief. She only cares for the child and that is all that matters now.

He will call his daughter Sophia. Her beauty touches his heart. Already, at one day old, he sees a resemblance to her mother. And his own hair, before it turned white, was dark like this. He is glad now that she is not a boy. She is the daughter he never had and he will teach her everything he knows. He will teach her that everything he knows is open to doubt, and that this is the only way to learn. And he will learn to listen to her questions. She will grow up free in spirit for she is not a child conceived in sin. She will not tremble in fear and wet herself in church. She is just a child – beautiful, and loved. That is the gift her mother has given her.

49

GERRIT

Fools grow without watering.

Jacob Cats, *Moral Emblems*, 1632

Gerrit is not going to touch a drop. He has plenty to celebrate: it is his last day working for Mr van Loos. Six weeks' wages he's owed plus, he hopes, a hefty tip. It is a nice sunny day; his bunions have stopped hurting. There is always something to celebrate, in Gerrit's view.

But he is not going to, not today. He has a job to do and he is going to do it. It is his duty. Mr van Loos has been a good employer: tolerant, easygoing and – when he has the money – generous with his tips. Gerrit is not going to let him down. He has done so in the past, he admits it. He recalls, with shame, certain episodes. The demon drink is to blame. It wipes everything out of his head – and, in truth, there wasn't a lot there in the first place. Once he has sobered up he is overcome with remorse, of course, and Jan always forgives him. He is a good man; Gerrit is not going to let him down.

Gerrit has crossed the city and found his way to the Sarphatistraat. He knocks on the door. Inside he hears children yelling. Mr van Hooghelande opens the door, just a slit.

'I've come for the package,' says Gerrit.

The man narrows his eyes suspiciously.

'The package for Mr van Loos.' Gerrit's voice is stern.

He is taking his mission seriously. 'The painter.'

Mr van Hooghelande disappears. Gerrit hears foot-steps descending some stairs, a key clanking, a door opening. Far away, echoing, there's another door opening and closing.

'Who are you?' A child is staring up at him.

'Gerrit.'

The child inserts its finger up its nostril and twists it round, as if unstopping a cork. 'There's monsters down there.'

'Where?'

'Down there. My pappa talks to them.'

More clanking and Mr van Hooghelande comes upstairs. He carries a small parcel. It is wrapped in brown paper and tied with string. He gives it to Gerrit, taps the side of his nose and closes the door.

Gerrit saunters off. Why did the man tap the side of his nose? Who are the monsters that live in his vault? Gerrit kicks a twig out of his way – the streets are still littered from last night's storm.

A drowned dog floats in the canal beside him. Bluish and matted, it is distended like a bladder. Poor *gek*, he thinks. That could be me, when I have had a skinful.

But he is not going to have a skinful, not today.

50

CORNELIS

How can a mother better expresse her love to her young babe, than by letting it sucke of her owne breasts? As this is a testimony of love, so it is a meanes of preserving and increasing love: for daily experience sheweth that mothers love those children best to whom they themselves give sucke.

William Gouge, *Of Domesticall Duties*, 1622

Cornelis says: 'We must engage a wet-nurse.'

'Oh, but I have,' replies Maria. 'I didn't want to trouble you, sir, and as I knew of one I took the liberty of engaging her services on your behalf.'

'Where is she?'

'She came at noon but she's gone now.'

'Did the baby suck?' he asks.

'Oh yes,' says Maria dreamily. 'Oh yes, she sucked all right. Hungry as a horse.'

'Who is this woman? When shall I see her? Have you prepared a room for her?'

Maria pauses. 'The problem is, sir, she's lame. It's a trial for her, walking here. So I thought I would just – well, take the baby there, when the little darling is hungry. We don't want the wet-nurse to keep your daughter at her lodgings, do we?'

'No! I want my Sophia here, in her home. You agree?'

'Oh yes, sir.' Maria nods. 'Her place is here, with us. I have grown very fond of her, sir.'

Cornelis feels a little confused. What happens if the baby wakes at night? However, Maria seems to understand the arrangement; she has taken charge and for this he is profoundly grateful. Besides, he has never had dealings with a wet-nurse before – Hendrijke fed their sons herself. If this is a usual measure, so be it. The important thing is to keep his daughter here. He has already lost everything else; he cannot lose his precious child to a stranger.

'We're her family now,' says Maria, lowering the baby into the crib.

Cornelis says: 'She has my nose, don't you agree?'

Maria's face is buried in the crib; she is nuzzling the baby. Her head moves, but he cannot tell if it is yes or no.

For the first time in months, Cornelis inspects his servant. She is essential to him now; she has stepped out of the wings into the centre of the stage and he feels a rush of affection for her.

'You look much diminished, my dear,' he says. 'All this sadness. You must eat and keep up your strength. We need you, Sophia and I.'

Sophia. Saying the name makes him feel strange. It is too soon to transfer all the love that is stored in that word to a new, tiny, empty vessel. He must give it time.

'I don't think she looks like anybody,' says Maria, raising her flushed face. She smiles – a dazzling smile. It quite startles him. 'She just looks like herself.'

❧ 51 ❧

GERRIT

Know – one false step is never retrieved.

Jacob Cats, *Moral Emblems*, 1632

Gerrit is making admirable progress. He has collected the pigments from the shop: umber, indigo and burnt sienna. He has visited the baker's shop. There were only two cinnamon pastries left, so, to make up the number, Gerrit has bought four vanilla ones too. Four and two makes six. See? He can do his sums. Now he is making his way back towards Jordaan, mission accomplished.

But, oh, his throat is dry. It has been a long day; he has been up since five this morning, unloading barrels. Thirsty work, and he hasn't touched a drop since breakfast. Bells are tolling the hour – two o'clock. He has a few coins left in his pocket. It seems wrong, somehow, to leave them there when they could bring him such relief. But he is managing.

Gerrit walks round a corner. He nearly bumps into his friend Piet, who is taking a piss outside the Lion.

'You old cock!' cries Piet, adjusting his breeches. 'You old tosspot! Come in for a jar. That old fornicator Andriesz's inside, he's had a win on the lottery.'

Gerrit hesitates.

'A hogshead of Rhenish, no less,' says Piet. 'Nobody's paying for drinks today.'

Gerrit stands there. This is torture. A roar of laughter

comes through the open door. He smells roasting fowl. He realizes that he is ravenously hungry; he hasn't eaten since five o'clock either, and then just a plate of porridge. It is truly a monumental struggle. Noble instincts pull him one way; temptation the other.

'What are you hanging about for?' asks Piet.

Gerrit shakes his head. 'Got to get back.'

Gerrit walks away on leaden legs. A tricky moment there, but he has done it. Duty has triumphed.

Doesn't he deserve a drink, as a reward? Gerrit, smiling grimly at his joke, walks towards the Bloemgracht, where his master waits.

❧ 52 ❧

SOPHIA

The maid is not dead, but sleepeth.

Matthew 9:24

I am not dead. I am merely sleeping, for what is our life but a long sleep from which we shall wake to the joyful trumpets of the Kingdom of Heaven?

These bedclothes are my shroud. When I rise it will be to a new life. I will break out, like a butterfly from a chrysalis; I will shed my past like Maria's cloak and disappear across the sea to my own Promised Land.

'Call that an arm!?'

Through my dreams I hear a voice. I will be re-assembled. My arms and legs, lying scattered, will rejoin my body and I will rise again from death, my own small resurrection.

'Call that a leg? Have you no eyes in your head?!'

Mattheus's voice floats up through the floorboards. He bellows loud enough to wake the dead.

'This is a head. It sits on the shoulders, am I correct? Two arms, one each side.' His studio is below this room; he must be giving a drawing lesson to his pupils. 'Have you no understanding of human anatomy at all? Know what your parents are paying, for you to waste my time like this?'

I have been sleeping for a long time. The storm is over; sunlight streams through the window. I will remain here, out of sight, until Jan comes to collect me. Mattheus and his wife are hiding me here in their house; they are sworn to secrecy. They are the only people alive who know the truth, apart from the doctor and the midwife who delivered me, for I am newly born too. The two men who carried me here assumed I was just a body. How roughly they handled me! Where is the respect? When life has departed we are nothing but a sack of turnips and I have the bruises to prove it. After all, our soul has flown.

'Bones! Muscles!' booms Mattheus through the floorboards. 'That's what's under our skin. If you can't understand how a body works, how on earth can you bloody paint it?'

I still cannot catch up with what has happened. Last night has the stagy unreality of a theatrical performance. It *was* a performance. We mouthed the words, we acted our parts. Much of the time I was alone, screaming my painless screams to nothing but my dusty bridal coronet that hung from the ceiling. My fellow actors were upstairs with Maria, working for real.

I tell myself: I will never set foot in that house again. I will leave my clothes in the closets, my tasks half finished, for I am dead.

The enormity of it has not yet hit me. The house is just a stage set from which, when the show was over, I slipped away into the night.

I do not want to think. Because once I do, I shall realize what I have done to my husband.

⋘ 53 ⋙

GERRIT

Where the knot is loose, the string slippeth.

Jacob Cats, *Moral Emblems*, 1632

Gerrit plods along the street. His legs ache; he has crossed the city once and now he is half-way back. Not far now, and he will be home. He will deliver the packages, Jan will pay him and then he will be a free man.

He hears, far away, the banging of a drum. Faint music floats in the air. The sound tugs him as if he is a bullock, pulled by a rope. He follows it and finds himself in the market square. A crowd has gathered. Clutching his packages, he eases his way through. He stops, entranced, and gazes at the scene.

A group of travelling entertainers has set up in the corner of the square. A man, dressed as Harlequin, juggles balls. Gerrit loves jugglers. Next to him a swarthy magician stands on a box, flourishing scarves. Gerrit loves magicians even more. The drum rolls. The magician shakes open a scarf: out flies a dove. The crowd roars. Gerrit's jaw drops.

The magician holds an egg in the palm of his hand. Grinning, he shows it to the crowd. He closes his hand. The drum rolls. He opens his hand. It's empty. Then he puts his hand behind his ear and – hey presto! – pulls out the egg.

The crowd roars louder. Gerrit stands there, his mouth hanging open. How does the fellow do it? It's magic! Gerrit's wits try to grapple with this; it is beyond his understanding. It is like these pigments, here in the parcel. Just lumps and crystals, that is all they are. Jan will make them disappear. He will transform them into trees. The sky!

Gerrit stands there, as enchanted as a child. There's another fellow, dressed as an Oriental. He's swallowing nails. *Nails*. Gerrit cannot bear to look. He squeezes his eyes shut and next moment, when he opens them, the man is blowing flames out of his mouth.

And then a donkey is dragged on. It is pitifully thin and wears a dunce's hood on its head. The man looks like a gypsy – wizened, with a flourishing moustache. He is dressed up as a teacher and carries a blackboard, which he props up in front of the donkey. He cracks his whip; the beast won't budge.

Gerrit stands, rooted to the spot. A cripple rattles his tin at him but he takes no notice. The man cracks his whip again.

'Time for class, Dobbin!'

The crowd titters. Gerrit is a simple, soft-hearted man. He loves all defenceless creatures – puppies, kittens. He especially loves donkeys – their big, furry heads, their ears. Maybe it's because he has been called a donkey himself; when Jan gets angry with him he calls him an ass.

The donkey refuses to go down on its knees. It stands there on its dainty hooves, its great head hanging. It looks so sad, its ears poking out of the holes in its hood. They move back and forth, separately.

'Time for your sums, Dobbin!' The man cracks his whip again. The donkey lifts up its head and brays – a noise of bottomless despair.

Suddenly the man loses his temper. He whips the donkey once, hard. The crowd titters. Then he starts whipping it in earnest – hard, stinging strokes.

Gerrit's eyes fill with tears. The poor dumb creature. The crowd is laughing now. How could they? The donkey stands there, rocked by the stings of the whip.

Something snaps. Gerrit drops his parcels and pushes through the crowd.

'That's not n-n-n-nice!' he bellows.

The man gazes at him. Gerrit grabs the whip out of the man's hand.

Like a showman, Gerrit flourishes the whip. It hisses above his head. The crowd gasps. Then – thwack! – he hits the donkey man. He whips the bastard harder and harder; the whip sings through the air. The man cowers, backing off, his hands over his face. The crowd roars louder.

And now Gerrit is chasing the donkey man across the square. The crowd applauds, pressing back to let him pass. The fellow zigzags around the stalls and vaults over a box of apples. Gerrit thunders after him in pursuit. The man sprints down an alley and is gone.

Suddenly, Gerrit is a hero. People are patting him on the back. He is being propelled into the nearby tavern. Voices jabber around him. 'You saw him off and no mistake!' Gerrit feels limp. He trembles with shock, for he is not a violent man. In fact, he has never hit anybody in his life.

Somebody sits him down at a table. 'He deserved it,' says a voice, 'the cowardly rascal!'

'It just didn't seem right,' mutters Gerrit modestly. 'Poor donkey . . . poor dumb creature. I'm a poor dumb creature but does my master beat me?'

There is an explosion of laughter. Gerrit blushes, pleased at his own wit. A tankard of beer is put in front of him.

'It's on the house.' A big, blowzy woman smiles at him.

'Just the one,' he says. 'Then I must be on my way.' He is still trembling; he can hardly lift the tankard to his lips.

'I heard the commotion,' says the woman. 'I saw what you did. Know something? I've buried two husbands and you're more of a man than both of them put together.'

Gerrit is gazing, mesmerized, at her breasts. *Both of them . . .* They are the largest breasts he has ever seen. They have a life of their own, shifting like creatures trying to get comfortable under her blouse. He gulps down his beer.

Other people join them. The lady tells them about Gerrit's valiant exploit.

Gerrit says: 'I'm a poor old donkey myself but does my master beat me?'

They roar with laughter all over again. He is hugely enjoying himself now.

A boy comes in. He puts three packages on the table. 'You dropped these,' he says.

Gerrit stares at them. Phew! That was a near miss. All this excitement, it has been wiped clean from his mind. He nearly lost them. Truly he *is* an ass.

He rises to his feet. 'I'd better be off.'

Someone sits him down again. Another brimming tankard is put in front of him.

❧ 54 ☙

JAN

By so much the more are we inwardly foolish, by how much we strive to seem outwardly wise.

Jacob Cats, *Moral Emblems*, 1632

There is a knock at the door. Thank God! Gerrit has returned.

Jan jumps to his feet and opens it. His landlord steps into the room.

'Oh,' says Jan.

'Just checking,' says the man. He is a skinny, shrewd fellow who lives in the next street.

'You too?' asks Jan. 'Think I'm going to leave without saying goodbye?'

'Just checking. Can't be too careful. Seeing as you owe me two months' rent. Seeing as – let's admit it – we've had some arrears in the past.'

Doctor Sorgh shifts in his seat. He darts a look in Jan's direction. He sighs, as if his suspicions were indeed well founded.

'You'll have the money by the end of the afternoon,' says Jan. 'So will these other gentlemen. I'll bring it round personally.'

'I think I'll wait here.' The landlord looks at the doctor and the boy, sitting there. 'I assume that's what you're doing too? May I join you?' He sits down.

'Gerrit will be here shortly,' says Jan. He adds

pathetically: 'He's bringing us cakes.' Where in God's name is his servant, the bumbling ass? He turns to the doctor. 'What time is it?'

Doctor Sorgh takes out his pocket watch. 'Ten minutes past three.'

❧ 55 ❧

GERRIT

The pot goeth so long to the water, til at last it commeth broken home.

Jacob Cats, *Moral Emblems*, 1632

Gerrit's head swims. Outside, apparently, the performers and the donkey have disappeared. It's magic – puff, and they're gone. Here in this smoky tavern, however, they have taken on the stuff of legend.

Word has passed from drinker to drinker. In the telling the donkey has grown smaller – *just a little mite, just a baby*. The man has grown into a monster of evil and now he is firmly believed to be a Spaniard.

Gerrit swells with pride. Apparently, now, the donkey is his own little country – so vulnerable, so brave. The Spaniard tries to beat it into submission. *Down*, he orders. *Down on your knees*! And along comes Gerrit the Brave, the toast of the tavern, the toast of the city, the toast of his people who struggle against their Popish invader.

It's heady stuff, being a hero. Gerrit says he's hungry and here, in front of him, the huge breasts hove into view. Mistress what's-her-name – she's told him but he cannot remember – she places in front of him a platter of smoked herring, bread and cheese.

Gerrit feels profoundly contented. Everybody is roaring drunk and so is he. He's told them his life story and they have drunk to that. He told them about when he was a child, how he worked a tread-wheel in a rope works; their eyes brimmed with tears. He told them about the time he fell through the ice; they roared with laughter. He told them about working for Jan van Loos. 'Five years I've served him and tomorrow I'm a free man.' They raise their glasses and drink to that. They are his orchestra and he is the conductor. And he has lost his stutter; the words flow from his lips.

Munching a mouthful of fish, he tries to remember that thing about magic. What did he think? It seemed clever at the time. He is a bit befuddled but if he tries hard . . . He doesn't want to lose his audience now.

'Magic, it's like this, see.' He picks up the package of pigments and fumbles open the string. 'Here's these lumps of colours . . . my master – hey presto! – he turns them into trees, into beautiful ladies . . .' Inside, there is an onion. He has opened the wrong parcel. He chuckles. 'Hey presto, it's an onion!'

Another roar of laughter. Magic, see? Actually, an onion is just what he fancies; he is partial to an onion with his herring. 'That's no onion,' says somebody, but Gerrit doesn't hear.

Somewhere behind him a fiddler strikes up a tune. People move away and start singing.

Gerrit picks up the knife and laboriously – he had better be careful, the knife's sharp – he peels off the skin. His hands refuse to obey him. Shaking with merriment, he admonishes them. 'Don't be dunces,' he tells them. Clumsily they are slicing up the onion. Today everything strikes him as hilarious – donkeys, onions, life.

He shovels in a mouthful of herring. Then, with the knife, he spears a round of onion and shoves it in too.

Mm . . . He's ravenous . . . as hungry as a horse, as hungry as a donkey . . . The attention has moved away from him but he doesn't mind. He concentrates on eating.

He sits there bent over his plate. He shovels in the onion and the herring; he tears off a piece of bread and stuffs that into his mouth too. Something tastes curious but he is too hungry to care. Mouth half full, he shoves in some more. He gobbles it all up and soon it is gone.

Look! Just like magic. His plate is empty.

Gerrit leans back in the settle and belches with satisfaction.

Sophia

Every sin carries its own punishment.

Jacob Cats, *Moral Emblems*, 1632

Lysbeth, Mattheus's wife, carries a pile of costumes into the room and heaps them on to the bed. I shall need something to wear for my journey down to the harbour; the luggage will be sent separately from Jan's house.

'You can choose a disguise,' says Lysbeth. 'They belong to my husband, he keeps them here for his clients. Some of them like dressing up for their portraits. A grocer down in the Rokin, he and his wife had themselves painted as the Archangel Gabriel and the Madonna.'

I could escape as the Virgin Mary! After all, she is accustomed to miracles. I blush at this blasphemous thought – I am not myself tonight – but no thunderbolt strikes me. And I have got away with worse.

Lysbeth sits down on the bed. 'It's so brave.' She sighs. 'Faking your death, eloping to the East Indies, and all for love.'

'I have done a terrible thing.'

'I do envy you,' she says. This sounds heartfelt. Mattheus isn't an easy man to live with. Outside the room, children thunder up and down the stairs. There are seven of them. Lysbeth bears them uncomplainingly, just as she patiently bears her husband's numerous infidelities and bouts of drunkenness. Jan has told me all about them. Mattheus lives a precarious life. His fortunes rise and fall – as well as painting, he deals in pictures and property, and makes some spectacular losses. Once, the bailiffs came to cart away their furniture and only left the bed because, at the time, Lysbeth was giving birth in it. She is a docile, long-suffering wife and she supports her husband through thick and thin. Mattheus invariably crawls home; she always forgives him for she is a real Christian, she does not finger her rosary mouthing lies, as I do.

I look at the heap of costumes. How shall I depart: as Pallas Athene? As a Jewish Bride? I can be a figment of my own imagination. If I were an angel I could fly to Batavia. They lie on the bed, the other selves I could become. The prospect is dizzying. I could become a creature of mythology, who never existed. No – who exists more vividly than the millions of us who simply die, uncelebrated in anyone's imagination.

How strange I feel today. It is hardly surprising. I have disappeared from the world. I have no idea what the future holds. What is Batavia? A jumble of syllables and a vision of eternal summer. The fog of Holland lifts like a curtain to reveal – what? I have thrown away everything – my marriage, my family, my life in that great house – for invisibility. For love.

Mattheus's voice booms up through the floorboards. 'Sit on his knee, dear! Arms around him – here – like this.'

The pupils have gone. Now Mattheus has hauled in some drunks from the local alehouse. According to Lysbeth he is painting his fifteenth *Peasants Carousing*.

Or is it *Merrymakers in a Brothel*? They are painted to give both enjoyment and moral instruction, depicting the disastrous consequences of inebriation and sensual indulgence. Mattheus has his favourite models, but they are often in a state of inebriation themselves. Judging by his voice, so is he. But he will get it painted; he is a true professional and besides, he has the stamina of an ox.

Time passes. Outside, the low winter sun has slipped behind the church. I wish Jan would come. He should have sold the bulb by now. I want to see him. I want to run my fingers over his face and know that he is alive. Until then I do not know if I am living or dead. Tonight is our last night in this country. I still cannot believe it.

A guffaw floats up through the floorboards. 'I said carousing,' yells Mattheus. 'Not bloody fucking!' There is a bellow of laughter.

Suddenly Lysbeth says: 'I'd cut off my right arm to keep him sober.'

She leaves, abruptly.

§ 57

Jan

He that lies down with dogs gets up with fleas.

Jacob Cats, *Moral Emblems*, 1632

It is six o'clock. A great flaming sunset, a sunset that suffused the sky with fire, has long since been extinguished. Darkness has fallen. In Jan's studio a small crowd has now gathered. Men sit on the bed; they lean against the wall smoking their pipes. Throughout the afternoon his creditors have gathered here one by one. Doctor Sorgh, the landlord and the boy from the East India Company have been joined by the butcher, the tavern keeper and a local loan shark, to all of whom Jan owes large sums of money. Each time there is a knock at the door Jan springs up: 'He's here!' But Gerrit has still not returned.

Food and drink have been brought in. At first glance it looks as if Jan is holding a party. There is, however, little conversation. Stony-faced, his creditors wait. They are going to sit it out. Doctor Sorgh takes out his pocket watch yet again and looks at it. The butcher leans against the wall, cracking his knuckles. They look like the grimmest of passengers waiting for a coach that will never arrive.

Outside in the street, another small crowd has gathered. Word has got around: Jan van Loos is taking delivery of the most valuable tulip bulb in the world. If rumour can be believed, its price today has risen sky high. Whispers pass from person to person. It is worth a chest full of gold; it is worth a ship filled with gold; it is worth a fleet of ships filled with gold; it is worth the entire contents of Stadholder Frederik Hendrik's Treasury. It is worth enough gold to feed every man, woman and child in the Republic for all their lives. It's worth all the gold of this Golden Age and then more.

'It's only a *bulb*,' someone says. 'They all look the same anyway. How can you tell?'

Indoors, Jan has taken refuge in the kitchen. He cannot bear to see his guests' faces and conversation has long since dried up. They are growing mutinous, he can feel it. They are, of course, doubting the existence of this bulb. They suspected he was lying to them and now their suspicions have hardened into certainty. They have been the victims of a colossal confidence trick and however much he has tried to reassure them – telling them that Gerrit will soon be back, that three groups of speculators are waiting at the Cockerel, ready to bid for the bulb – however much he tells them that soon they will have the money in their hands he knows that their faith in him – tenuous at the best of times – has drained away.

Jan sits there, gazing at a pile of fingers; he dropped the plaster arm during packing and swept the bits into the corner. How could he have entrusted Gerrit with the bulb? The man is a half-wit. No – it is Jan himself who is the idiot. He should have insisted on going himself. He could have dragged the doctor with him. He must have been mad.

Sophia must be getting worried. He has hardly had

time to think about her; she has faded into the background. Her death, though feigned, seems somehow to have removed her from the drama of the living. She will be waiting for a message that he has cashed in the bulb and discharged his debts; she will be awaiting his arrival. He is due to spend the night with her at Mattheus's house before they set sail at dawn. Lysbeth is cooking them a celebratory goose.

And then Jan hears it: the faint sound of singing. He goes into the studio and hurries to the window. It is very faint, but it's heading this way. He recognizes it as a parent, through a jabber of voices, knows the voice of his child.

'Come all you maidens fair
That are just now in your prime . . .'

The voice grows nearer. In the street, the crowd titters and moves aside. Gerrit lumbers out of the darkness.

'I'll have you keep your gardens clean
And let no man steal your thyme . . .
With a heigh da-di-do and a hey da-di-di . . .'

Gerrit staggers, recovers himself and heads for the front door.

Jan flings it open. Gerrit stumbles in.

'Where in God's name have you been?' demands Jan. 'I told you to come straight home!'

'I been . . .' Gerrit's speech is slurred. 'I been . . . fighting the Spanish . . .' One arm is folded over his chest, protecting something. He waves his other arm wildly in the air. 'Swish swish! . . . I fought them and I won.' He gazes, blinking, at the men in the room. 'Hello. Having a party? Can I join in?'

'No,' says Jan. 'We are not having a party. We are waiting for you.' He sits Gerrit down on a chair. 'Where is the package?' He speaks slowly, as if to the deranged. 'The packages I asked you to collect. Where are they?'

'Got them here.' Gerrit opens his jerkin, proudly, and pulls out two paper parcels. They are battered by now; the string is coming loose. 'Got them, just like you said.'

He passes them to Jan. Jan takes the parcels to the table. The men stare, mesmerized. There is no sound except for Gerrit's wheezing lungs; he is breathing heavily from his exertions.

Jan unties the first package. Inside lie lumps of pigment, loosely wrapped in tissue paper.

There is a silence. Jan opens the other package. There are crumbs and broken bits of pastry.

'Sorry, sir,' mumbles Gerrit. 'G-G-Got a bit . . . knocked about a bit . . . fighting, see . . . fighting the Spanish . . .'

Jan whispers: 'Where is the tulip bulb?'

Gerrit looks at him; his mouth hangs open. 'The what?'

'The third package, Gerrit. It had a tulip bulb in it.'

'The onion? I ate it.'

❧ 58 ❧

SOPHIA

If you peel an onion, you cry.

Jacob Cats, *Moral Emblems*, 1632

I have a nosebleed.

'I get them too, when I'm agitated,' says Lysbeth. She is ironing a dress for me to wear. She brings over the hot iron. 'Here, lean over this. Let a few drops fall on it, that'll do the trick.'

I lean over the iron. The drops of blood land with a sizzle. Suddenly I miss Maria and her superstitions. We have been through so much together, more than anyone will ever know, and I will never see her again. I will never find out if she and the baby are thriving. Will her ruse work, the ruse about the wet-nurse? Will the baby's resemblance to Maria become too apparent? These are questions I can no longer ask. Death has removed me from the living and soon I will leave this country for good.

I feel lonely. The only person to whom I have spoken is this woman Lysbeth, whom I have never met before. Where is Jan? I fling back my head and press a handkerchief into my nostrils. The iron didn't cure my nosebleed. I am full of blood; I am too much alive.

Why isn't he here? Outside, the church bells peal eight o'clock. Lysbeth goes downstairs to baste the goose. I take out my rosary beads – I was clutching them in my hand when I died, they are all I have with me. '*Hail Mary,*

Mother of God . . .' I count the beads, praying for him to come. It feels wicked, to pray for our treachery to succeed, but I am past redemption now.

At least my nosebleed has stopped. I take off my nightdress and put on the clothes Lysbeth has laid out for me – a shift, a petticoat and a black dress and bodice. I have decided not to wear an exotic disguise; I am not in the mood for any more pantomimes. I shall wear plain black, and the blue cloak that the grocer's wife wore when she was the Madonna.

I sit on the bed, waiting. Outside there is a roar, and childish shrieks. Mattheus is chasing his children up and down the stairs.

'I'm the bogeyman! I'm coming to get you!' he bellows.

Lysbeth calls up to him: 'Don't excite them. They won't eat their dinner.'

Footsteps thunder along the passage and then there is silence. Somewhere outside, far away, a dog barks. I feel cut off from this boisterous family, from life itself. In Utrecht my mother and sisters will be grieving. I cannot bear to think of their tears. I have left Cornelis a note instructing him, in the event of my death, to continue supporting them, but though this may ease their circumstances it will not heal their sorrow. Not far from here, in the house in the Herengracht, Cornelis will be mourning his dead wife. How can I do this to them? How can I be so cruel, to sacrifice their happiness for my own? I can sail to the ends of the earth, but they will remain for ever in my guilty heart.

Outside, the church bells toll the quarter. My hands are trembling as I smooth the blue cloak over my knees.

Jan should be here by now. What is happening? He has sent no message, nothing.

The house seems strangely quiet. Even Mattheus's booming voice has stopped. I do not dare to leave this room; the children must not see me.

And then I hear footsteps on the stairs. They are slow, heavy footsteps; the tread of an elderly man.

It is Cornelis. He has opened the coffin and found it filled with sand. He has discovered my deceit.

The stairs creak, as loud as pistol shots, as he approaches. Surprisingly, I stay calm. In fact, a curious feeling of relief spreads through me. It is all over.

The door opens and Jan steps into the room.

He looks terrible. His face is grey; he seems to have shrunk. He sits down on the bed – no greeting, nothing.

He says: 'We are ruined.'

It takes me a while to understand what he is telling me. It is something about Gerrit eating the bulb. What on earth is Jan talking about? He says they have taken everything.

'Who?'

'My creditors. They've taken my paintings, my chests, everything.' He pauses. 'They want to take out a charge against me. The doctor can't – if he does, it will all be revealed, what he's done – but the others may do so. My assets aren't worth enough to cover my debts. Not a quarter of them.'

It is only then that he takes my hand. He pulls me down beside him on the bed and kneads my fingers.

'I'm so very sorry, my love. I was a fool. But how can even a fool predict something so preposterous?'

There is a silence. 'What we did was worse than preposterous,' I say.

We sit there, side by side. I am thinking of our wickedness – our profound and unpardonable wickedness. God was watching us all the time. I knew He was, in my heart.

'We did something very terrible –' I begin.

'Listen, my darling –'

'We did it,' I say. 'And we have been punished.'

'We love each other.' He grabs my chin and turns my face to his. '*We love each other*. That's why we started all this, don't you remember?'

I cannot reply. I gaze at his face – his blue, glittering eyes; his madman's hair.

'You have died,' he says. 'We cannot stay in Amsterdam, we've got to get away. We can still do it. We'll have to start all over again, with nothing, but we can do it. Can you live with me in poverty?'

I do not listen. *Let me kiss her*, Cornelis cries as he is pulled away from my body. Far away, in the darkness, my mother has lost her daughter.

'We'll manage, my sweetheart.' Jan speaks with passion. 'We can still sail tomorrow, all is not lost. I'll ask Mattheus to lend us the money for our passage and I will pay him back when I've found employment . . . by all accounts there's plenty of work out there . . .' He clutches my shoulders. 'Do not despair, my only darling.'

God has been watching us all the time. God is all-seeing. I knew that, of course, I was just blinded by my own greed. God has done this to punish us.

Jan is looking at me, reading my thoughts. 'God will pardon us. Don't have doubts, Sophia. Not now.'

We sit there in silence. Outside, the dog is barking. A

smell of cooking drifts up the stairs. I cannot speak. It all makes sense; it was only a matter of time. There is a terrible symmetry to it: we committed the crime and for this we must be punished. God has driven Gerrit – bumbling, drunken Gerrit – to do His work. It has all fallen into place.

There is a long pause. My mind is made up. I turn to Jan, put my arms around him and kiss him deeply. How passionately he responds, with what relief. I dig my fingers into his hair and cradle his face in my hands. How I have loved him.

Our bodies are pressed together, but bodies tell their own lies. Mine has lied so often in the past. I hold Jan close, drinking in his kisses as if I will never stop. I am betraying him now, just as all those months we have been betraying others.

Then I ease myself out of his arms. 'Go and ask him, then,' I say, stroking his hair. 'Go and ask Mattheus to lend us the money. I will wait for you here.'

❧ 59 ❧

JAN

Love laughs at locksmiths.

Jacob Cats, *Moral Emblems*, 1632

Mattheus and Lysbeth are waiting in the kitchen. The goose turns on the spit. Drops of fat fall from it, hissing in the flames. Their spaniel watches, strings of saliva hanging from its mouth.

When Jan comes in Mattheus rallies. He pours him a glass of brandy and puts his arms around him. 'You poor old rogue,' he says. 'You've always been a fool when it comes to women.'

'She's not women.'

'So what are you going to do now?'

Jan drains the glass. 'We can still sail tomorrow, but we need your help.'

He asks for a loan. Mattheus agrees.

Lysbeth takes Jan's hand. 'We're glad to be of help. Soon you will be gone, and you can put all this behind you.'

At this moment their eldest son, Albert, wanders in.

'Time for your dinner,' says Lysbeth. 'Call the others.'

'Who's that woman?' asks the boy.

'What woman?' asks Jan.

'That woman who came running down the stairs,' says Albert. 'In the blue cloak. Is she a model?'

'Where is she?'

'She's gone.'

≈§ 60 §≈

SOPHIA

None can clean their dress from stain, but some blemish will remain.

Jacob Cats, *Moral Emblems*, 1632

There is a full moon tonight. No painter can reproduce the perfection of God's work; what presumption to try! The moon is a perfect circle, more perfect than the orbs that Jan painted in his moonlit landscapes, more perfect than the rows of greedy 'O's that he drew when he was hunched over his sums . . . those empty 'O's that led us to this.

The streets are deserted. They are bathed in ghostly light as I run through them, my slippers pit-patting. For once I do not care if I am seen, for I have reached my final surrender. Last night I died to the world, but tonight I shall disappear for good. The relief makes me light-footed; I skim along.

The moon, reflected in the water, accompanies me. The heavens have fallen; in one convulsion my world has been turned upside down. No wonder that print haunted me when I was little, that drowned world where the bells tolled underwater and the dead swayed. I thought that their arms waved in supplication; now I realize that they waved in greeting. I knew that I would arrive here in the end.

The waters of this city mirror us back to ourselves – the vanity of it! Maria dressed up in my clothes; she gazed in the mirror and dreamed herself as me. My own vanity is far more profound. I have presumed to turn the natural order inside-out. I have meddled with God's plan; my pride is the pride of our people who wrenched our country from the sea. *The making of new land belongs to God alone*, wrote one of our engineers, Andries Vierlingh, *for He gives to some people the wit and strength to do it*. What double-thinking is this? We use God to justify our actions when in fact it is our own instinct for survival that pushes us on.

But why survive? This world is but a chimera, a dazzling reflection. Did we suspect this, when we built our city upon mirrors? Once I dreamed of a life with Jan. I gazed into the water and saw a dream world, mirroring my own, where I could be happy. How wrong I was. For it was nothing – just the glitter of moonlight on the surface, the sheeny satin lustre of a dress. That was all it ever was. Through lust and pride, those deadly sins, I blinded myself to the truth.

Tonight I shall bid goodbye to this optical illusion. I shall disappear from this world and truly be reborn, for Jesus waits for me, His arms outstretched like a lover. And nobody, not even my darling Jan, will be able to find me. *There's only one way to escape*, we said, all those months ago, *and for him never to think to look for me*.

I am standing on a bridge now. I look down at the pewtery sheen of the water. I think of all the things I have loved in this world: my sisters, flowers with dewdrops trembling in their freckled throats ... the smell of clean linen, the smell of a horse's neck, when I bury my face in its fur ... the taste of warmed wine as Jan poured it from his mouth into mine, of his skin against my lips ... I remember the first night we lay together, our fingers laced, gazing at each other with terrible seriousness ... in our end was our beginning, for we knew in our hearts that we were doomed ...

There is no time to lose. He will be searching for me now and I have not gone far – just a few streets from Mattheus's house. I lean over the parapet, gazing at the moon's reflection. Like my own face, it gazes up at me. *Vanity of vanities, all is vanity* ...

I pull off my cloak and drop it over the edge. It floats on the water – my last, shed skin.

ᏼ 61 ᏾

WILLEM

What waters are not shadowed by her sails?
On which mart does she not sell her wares?
What peoples does she not see, lit by the moon,
She who herself sets the laws of the whole ocean?

Joost van den Vondel

Down in the port, six ships of the fleet have docked. Crowds of sailors pour down the gangways, setting foot in their homeland for the first time in months. Some fall to their knees and kiss the ground, thanking God for their safe return; others head for the stews. The sea front seethes with activity – relatives, pickpockets and whores mill around the new arrivals. Hawkers shout their wares. Lights glow in the waterside taverns; the brothels throb with music.

A young man weaves his way through the crowd. He carries his belongings in a bag, slung over his shoulder. The flames of a brazier illuminate his face. Eight months at sea have transformed Willem. He has lost his puppy fat; his face is lean and brown. He walks with confidence. The sea has made a man of him – a fine young man, tall and upstanding, though the streets still roll beneath his feet. He is not the same Willem who left in March, battered, beaten and stripped of his illusions. He has lost his innocence – that will never return. However, something more profound has taken its place: wonder.

228

The sights he has seen! Mountains, for a start. He is a Dutchman, he has never seen such things before. Who could believe they could be so steep? He has seen waves as high as mountains and mountains so tall they must be scraping heaven. He has seen whales the size of mountains, whales hoving into sight, water spouting through their blowholes, water sluicing off their sides, whales plunging into the depths, a moment of stillness and then their great tails rearing up and following them. He has seen shooting stars in a spangled southern sky; he has seen flying fish glittering like silver arrows. He has seen cities to dream about: the gleaming domes of Constantinople; the ravishing, mirrored streets of Venice, corrupt and seductive, like Amsterdam's wanton sister.

Willem has both seen wonders and caused wonder in others. After his first disastrous encounter with a whore he has made up for lost time and the reaction has been gratifying. In three languages women of easy virtue have marvelled at his astonishing member. (*Wat heb je een grote lul!* . . . *Che grozzo kazzo!* . . . *Ku kuzegar o khar o kuze faroush!*) It has done battle and so has he. He has battled against storms in the Bay of Biscay, scaling the rigging and lashing the ropes. He waged war against the fever and survived. Most gratifying of all, he has fought the Spanish and has a full purse to prove it.

For Willem has gold in his pocket. Not the fool's gold that fattened his purse the last time he walked these streets – this is real cash, plundered in a spirit of patriotism. While engaged on escort duty to a merchant fleet sailing to the Levant, his ship was attacked by a Spanish vessel. After a fierce engagement the Dutchmen captured the ship, plundered its cargo and divided up the spoils. His captain and fellow crewmen have taken their percentage of the bullion.

It is not surprising that Willem feels a profound gratitude to the sea. She has yielded up two livelihoods: her fish and then her gold. With this booty, plus his wages, he has enough cash to discharge himself from the navy and start a new life. His expectations are still modest. A little shop, he would be happy with that. Not fish, however; he is sick of fish. He wants to set up in a little cheese shop, with Maria at his side.

All these months he has tried to forget her but he cannot do so; she is lodged in his body like lead shot. Maria has made him a chronic invalid. Maybe the wound has healed but she lies beneath his skin; the slightest movement inflames the pain. He misses her desperately. The bitterness is still there, it has eaten away at his heart but it has failed to destroy his love for her. She is his soul mate; it is as simple as that. With rented arms around him it was Maria to whom he made love; it was through her eyes that he marvelled at the minarets of Alexandria.

He misses her chuckling laugh and her chapped hands, her robust good humour and sudden lapses into dreaminess. He misses her body. He has travelled the world but its centre of gravity lies between her sheets. *East or west, home is best.* He is a Dutchman, through and through.

Maria might be married; she might have left Mr Sandvoort's employment and gone to live with the man in whose passionate embrace Willem last saw her. She might have forgotten all about him. Of course he has thought of this, every hour of every day, but it will not deter him from trying to find her. He is a grown man, now, with money in his pocket. He has faced worse foes than this. And if he loses the battle and finds that she no longer loves him ... this is something he cannot contemplate, not tonight.

The houses of the Herengracht loom up in the moonlight. The bells toll eight; Willem smells cooking. Behind their shutters the families will be eating their dinners. How strange, yet familiar, these houses seem. In his former life he has knocked on their doors. *Fresh cod! Fresh haddock!* Such a journey he has made, through such storms, and to them it is simply a night like any other. Under his feet the street still sways with the swell of the sea. He has dreamt about returning here for so many months that he can hardly believe it is happening; he will wake up and find he is still swaying in his hammock on his rocking ship. The moon accompanies him in the water, his light of navigation.

He reaches the house. His heart beats faster. For a moment his courage fails him. Maria was his friend, that is the terrible thing, she was his dearest companion and now he dreads to see her. He shifts the bag on to his other shoulder and walks up to the front door. The window shutters are open. He looks through the glass.

In the front room an oil lamp glows on the table. The chairs are covered with black cloth and the paintings are turned to face the wall.

Willem stands, rooted to the spot. The blood drains from his body. Maria has died. He knows this is a stupid reaction. She is a servant; her death would not plunge a house into mourning. Besides, she is too young to die. The idea is unthinkable. The world, however, is full of strangeness. He can presume nothing any more.

It is, of course, the old man who has passed on. That is the obvious explanation. It must be recent. Maria and her mistress will be in mourning – if, that is, Maria still lives in the house. She has probably married and moved away months before. She may not even know that her old employer has died.

All this passes through Willem's head as he knocks on the door – diffidently, as a sign of respect. A long time passes. He knocks again, more loudly this time.

Finally he sees movement inside the house. A flickering candle appears in the front room. Willem presses his nose against the window-pane. The old man, wearing his cap and dressing-gown, looms out of the darkness and shuffles across the room. The candle-light burnishes his beard. There is the grind of bolts, then the sound of a key. The door is opened.

Willem gathers his wits. 'I am sorry to disturb you, sir. I have come to see Maria. Is she still in your employment?'

The old man peers at him. 'Who are you?'

'I am Willem. I used to sell you fish. She is an acquaintance of mine.' He tries to swallow. 'She is not dead, is she?'

Mr Sandvoort stares at him. 'No.' He shakes his head. 'No, she is not dead. Follow me.'

Willem closes the door behind him and follows Mr Sandvoort across the parlour, through the back room and down the passage. The old man pauses. 'No,' he says. 'It was my wife who died.'

'Your wife?'

Willem, stumbling on the steps, follows him down into

the kitchen. Warmth and a smell of cooking greet him. The table is laid for two. Maria sits in the corner, washing a baby.

She straightens up and stares at him. 'Willem!'

Her face lights up, then her expression hardens. Willem looks from her to the baby. For a mad moment he thinks that the baby belongs to her and the old man – the scene looks so domestic, almost as if they are married. His head spins.

Maria rises to her feet. Her eyes are narrowed to slits. The baby dangles from her hands as if she is holding up a prize salmon. She starts wrapping it in a cloth.

'What are you doing here?' she asks coldly.

'I came to see you.'

She looks at his clothes. 'Where have you been?'

'I joined the navy,' he says. 'We docked tonight.'

Mr Sandvoort addresses Maria. 'Are you all right, my dear?'

She nods and sits down heavily. Willem perches on a chair. He feels unwelcome but he is not going to leave, not yet. He must say something to the old man. 'I am so sorry, sir, that your wife passed away.'

'She died in childbirth,' says Maria. 'This is her baby. Her name is Sophia.'

'Ah.' Willem feels uncomfortable. Maria is still looking at him coldly, through narrowed eyes. She doesn't look pleased to see him at all. There is no ring on her finger but that proves nothing. She might be carrying on with this man illicitly; after all, she did the same thing with Willem. He feels a stab of pain. How rosy she looks in the firelight!

Mr Sandvoort clears his throat. 'Shall I leave you with

this young man, Maria? You will be safe?'

Maria nods. She is still looking at Willem. Mr Sandvoort leaves the room. They listen to his steps, shuffling away.

'Why did you leave me?' Maria blurts out. 'How could you do such a thing?'

'Me? What about you?'

'Why did you do it?'

'Because I saw you,' he replies. 'With that man.'

'What man?'

'You know who I mean.'

'What man?' Her voice rises. 'What man? Where?'

'I followed you that night. I saw you kissing.'

'Kissing? What do you mean?'

'Don't lie, Maria –'

'What are you talking about? I don't understand you. Why have you come here, after all these months, if you're just going to shout at me?'

'I'm not shouting!'

Her eyes fill with tears. 'I thought you loved me.'

'Of course I loved you!'

'That was why you left me, was it? Because you loved me? You broke my heart, Willem.' She starts to cry.

'All right,' he says. 'If you love me, come away with me.'

'What?'

'Come away with me, now.'

'Now?'

'Marry me.'

'But, Willem –'

'You think I'm not rich enough? I'm not as rich as he is?'

'As *who* is?' she yells.

'I've got money – you want money, I've got money.'
He fumbles in his pocket.

'I don't want money. What's the matter with you?'

'Show me you love me. Tell me you'll come away with me.'

'I cannot.'

'See? You don't love me.'

'Willem, I can't leave! I've got the baby.'

'Get a nurse.'

'I cannot. I have to stay here with the baby. You don't understand.'

'Oh, I understand all right –'

'You *don't*!' she shouts.

The baby starts crying.

Maria, her face pink, picks her up. 'I cannot leave her because she's mine.'

'What?'

'She's mine, you dolt. She's mine, she's ours. She's *yours*!'

The baby yells. Maria stares, distraught, at Willem. The baby is screaming now.

Maria unlaces her bodice. Her blouse falls from her shoulders. She puts the baby to her breast.

Willem stares at her as she suckles the child. Tiny fingers press at her flesh, as if playing a tune. The baby's damp curls, plastered to its head, are shockingly black against Maria's white skin. In the stunned silence he can hear a moist sound as the infant sucks; it is a secret, greedy sound, a sound of focused intensity. He has heard it before, with puppies. His mind works laboriously; he is trying to count back the months. Neither of them hears the door opening.

'Are you all right, my dear? All that shouting –'

Cornelis stops, in the doorway, and stares at Maria. The crying has ceased. In the candle-light Maria is naked to the waist. The old man stares at his baby, drinking at her breast.

❧ 62 ❧

JAN

*Hear my prayers, o Lord, and let my crying come unto
Thee. Hide not Thy face from me in the time of my trouble.*

Psalm 102

Jan, Lysbeth and Mattheus have been searching the streets in three different directions. They are searching at random because nobody can guess where Sophia has gone. Lysbeth suggested she might have returned to her home in the Herengracht, to give herself up and beg her husband's forgiveness. Jan cannot believe she would do such a thing. Mattheus has suggested she might be heading back to her family in Utrecht, but Jan cannot believe she would do this either.

He hardly listens to their speculations because he knows what Sophia is going to do. That is the terrible thing. He knows her through and through, he knows her inside out. There is only one thing left to her now and it will just be a matter of time before he finds that he is right.

Though what satisfaction can there be in being proved correct? When he returns to the house he finds Mattheus is already there. On the floor lies a sodden blue cloak.

'I found it in the canal,' says Mattheus. 'I pulled it out with a stick.'

He says that there was no sign of a body.

237

'We can go back and look,' he says. 'But how can we order the canal to be dragged? How can we look for somebody who is already presumed to be dead?'

❦ 63 ❧

CORNELIS

For I have eaten ashes as if it were bread; and mingled my drink with weeping.

Psalm 102

Cornelis is in a state of shock. He has suffered many blows in his life but now he feels as if his vital organs have been removed from his body. His frame barely supports him. Willem has poured him a glass of brandy, but Cornelis's hand is trembling and he cannot raise it to his lips.

His wife is alive. She has faked her death so that she can run away with the painter Jan van Loos.

The words sound so unreal; they cannot sink into his brain. Maria is explaining it all over again. 'Don't be angry with me, sir . . .' Her words echo, far away. 'I know it was wicked, as wicked as anything can be, but please don't punish me.'

Should he be angry with her? He supposes so.

Sophia has cheated him in a manner beyond all comprehension. He must be dreaming. He has fallen asleep in his chair. He will wake up to the simple grief of mourning.

No person on earth would inflict this suffering on another person. What desperation could have driven her to it? She was his *wife*.

She *is* his wife. She is alive. She is in the arms of this

man, somewhere, she is living and breathing. They are laughing at him. *The stupid old fool. What an idiot he is!* They are kissing and nuzzling . . .

'Where has she gone?'

'I cannot say, sir.'

'Where have they gone?' Cornelis shouts. The baby wakes and starts crying.

'I shouldn't have told you anything,' wails Maria. 'She'll kill me.'

'I'm going to find her.'

'Don't, sir. She has gone away. You will never find her, sir. It's best to think she is dead.'

Cornelis gets to his feet.

'Where are you going?' Maria asks, alarmed.

Cornelis looks at the baby. Her little face is brick-red; she is drawing breath for another yell. He wants to slot his finger into her mouth, to pacify her, but this suddenly seems too intimate. After all, she is not his child. Instead, he touches her cheek. 'And I thought she was mine,' he says. 'I thought she bore my nose.'

Cornelis hurries through the streets. Far away the ten o'clock trumpet sounds. The citizens of Amsterdam have shut themselves away for the night. How safe it once seemed, to blow out the candles and retire from the world. He is hurrying along the route his wife must have taken, on the way to her lover. A rat slips across the street and slides into the water. The canal stinks. Once he thought his city was so scrubbed, so safe, but she is rotten through and through. She is built on shaky wooden piles, which sink into the mud. These thin, narrow houses are just façades, as flimsy as paper; their faces are painted like whores, but what goes on within their long interiors? How easily these streets can all collapse and slide back into the slime; how could he have misled himself, all these years?

One nightmare has been replaced by another. The horror of Sophia's death has been succeeded by the greater horror of her being alive. The enemy did not lie outside his front door – it was not thieves, it was not the Spanish – the enemy lay within his own home. For how long had she been lying to him? When did she see this man – when Cornelis was at his work? Those evenings when she pleaded toothache or headache, did she flit through these streets then? Was she dreaming of him when Cornelis lay with her in bed, his arms around her? The treachery of this is too much to be borne but it is worse – she has watched his pride as her belly swelled, she has smiled at his joy as she patted her padded stomach. And all the time she has been devising the most fiendish plan to deceive him. What a fool she must think he is; what a cuckolded idiot.

Cornelis hurries through the streets of Jordaan. His lungs are bursting. His legs buckle under him but still he runs, his breath wheezing like bellows. He arrives at the Bloemgracht and stops outside the painter's house. There is no sign of life. He gazes at the closed shutters on the ground floor. Behind those shutters he stood in the studio proudly gazing at his own portrait. He paid eighty florins to the very man who was ravishing his wife. The bed was in the room, near enough to touch.

Cornelis batters at the door. There is no answer. He suspected this, but he had to come here – he has no idea where else to go.

Something stirs in the darkness. It appears to be a body, curled up in the gutter.

Cornelis bends down. The man blearily raises his head. It is the painter's servant.

'Where have they gone?' demands Cornelis.

The moonlight shines on the man's white face. It gapes at him. 'W-w-who?'

'You know whom I mean. Your master, Jan van Loos. Where has he gone?'

The man's moon-face gapes. 'I c-cannot say.'

'Tell me!' shouts Cornelis.

The fellow flinches, as if he is going to be hit. Cornelis takes some coins out of his purse. He drops them on the body; they land soundlessly The man turns away, his face against the wall.

'Tell me where they have gone.'

The man is muttering.

'What is it?' demands Cornelis. 'You want more money?'

The servant shakes his head. He mumbles something. 'Speak up!'

'I've d-done him wrong, sir. I've done him wrong once, I'm not going to make it worse. I beg you, sir – g-g-go away. Leave me alone.'

The man pulls his cloak over his head. Whimpering, he curls up. He looks like a dog who refuses to budge from his master's corpse.

Cornelis is overcome by fatigue. He lowers himself to the ground, next to the shuddering bundle. The man appears to be sobbing.

Cornelis, too, is an outcast. The walls that have

surrounded him have been removed, brick by brick, and he is utterly alone. What can he do now? There is nobody to whom he can turn for help. Even the Lord can no longer offer him guidance.

Shivering, Cornelis slumps against the wall. Down the street, men are stumbling out of a tavern. They shout their good-nights into the darkness.

He raises his head. He thinks: there was a boy. In the studio that day, there was a boy in the room – thin, pale . . . The man's apprentice. He stood next to them as they looked at the painting. *It is finely rendered, is it not? Your legs in particular* . . .

Who would know where to find him? Down the street a light is extinguished. The alehouse is closing for the night. Cornelis, his joints aching, climbs to his feet.

❧ 64 ❧

JACOB

*O my God, make them like unto a wheel: and as the
    stubble before the wind;*
*Like as the fire that burneth up the wood and as the flame
    that consumeth the mountains.*
*Persecute them even so with Thy tempest; and make them
    afraid with Thy storm.*
Make their faces ashamed, o Lord . . .

Psalm 83

In the Street of Knives the shutters are closed. The tools
of slaughter and dismemberment are locked away, safe
for the night, within the darkened cabinets. Upstairs the
shopkeepers and their wives lie sleeping. They dream of
the tight, silver belly of a herring. The knife slits it from
gills to anus; the guts spill out. They dream that their
fingers slide under a chicken's skin, sliding in like fingers
into a glove. The knife pierces the flesh; it eases in and
loosens the thigh from the carcass. Night after night they
dream of butchery, for this is their small world and they
know no other. All day, across the alley, the cleavers glint
at their fellow blades.

In Jacob's parents' shop, however, a light glows in the
back room. Surrounded by six candles and an oil lamp,
Jacob is preparing to paint. It is a big canvas and his
theme is an ambitious one: *The Expulsion of Adam and Eve
from the Garden of Eden*. Jacob is drawing the preliminary

sketch. Jan's wooden mannekin is propped in front of his easel. On his last day, in a small act of rebellion, Jacob stole it from the studio. He has posed the jointed doll in a posture of shame – head thrust forward, arm shielding the face. Eve will have her arms upraised in despair.

Jacob still seethes with fury at his own expulsion. The treachery of it! His master has blighted his career before it has even begun – how can Jacob pass his examination with nobody to teach him? Next week he will start tramping round other painters' studios but why should he be reduced to this? Jan has ruined Jacob's future to slake his own foul lust. He has even painted the woman. When he was alone, Jacob pored over the canvases – Sophia's breasts, her long white body . . . It made his body break out in sweat. He wants to take up one of these meat cleavers and hack the licentious bastard to pieces.

Jacob picks up his chalk and starts drawing. He bites his lip in concentration. Adam's stooped back; his wretched, naked buttocks . . . the face, glimpsed behind the shielding arm, will be a portrait of Jan, for it is his turn to suffer.

Someone is knocking at the door. Jacob lifts his head. Who could it be, at this hour?

Jacob hurries through the shop and unbolts the door of the shop. Mr Sandvoort stands there. He looks highly distressed – sweating, gasping for breath.

'Where has he gone?'

Jacob leads him into the back room and sits him down. 'Would you like a drink, sir?'

Mr Sandvoort shakes his head. Jacob knows who he is, of course. He is the husband of Jan's mistress, the woman who at this very moment is packing up to leave the country.

'How did you know I live here?' asks Jacob.

'What?' The old man seems distracted. 'Oh, I asked at the tavern.' He leans forward in the chair. His skin is grey and damp, his eyes feverish. 'You must help me, young man. You are the only person who can help me. Where has he gone?'

'Who?' asks Jacob, though he knows perfectly well.

'Your master, the painter Jan van Loos. He has disappeared with . . .' Mr Sandvoort swallows. 'I have reason to believe . . . it's imperative that I find out their whereabouts.'

Jacob doesn't reply. His mind is working fast.

'I will pay you handsomely,' pleads Mr Sandvoort.

'I do not want your money,' says Jacob with dignity.

'Do you know where they have gone? Were you – conversant with what was happening?'

Jacob nods.

'I beg you – please – tell me where I can find them.'

Jacob does not smile. Within him, however, he feels the warmth spreading. It is the warmth of deepest satisfaction. There is, indeed, sense to the world. The wicked shall be punished, for now he can ruin the man who ruined him.

'I know where they have gone.' Jacob pauses, enjoying his feeling of power. 'A boy came with the tickets.' He pauses again for the full effect. He holds Mr Sandvoort in his thrall. In a moment Jacob will destroy his former master and justice will be done. 'They are sailing to Batavia.'

'Batavia?'

'At first light tomorrow. On the *Empress of the East*.' As he speaks, Sophia's rosy nipples swim in front of his eyes. He feels a surge of chivalry. It fights with his jealousy and lust; after a short struggle, it wins. 'It is not your wife's fault, sir. She is not the one to blame. My master persuaded her to do it.' She, too, has been deluded by this wicked man; her virtue has been destroyed by him, just as he destroyed Jacob's career. 'She didn't mean you any harm, I am sure. I watched them, I should know. He persuaded her to do it against her better judgement.'

Mr Sandvoort thanks him. Turning to leave, he knocks against a cabinet. The knives rattle. And then he is gone.

Jacob returns to his painting. He gazes with satisfaction at the chalk figure, bowed with shame. Let Jan take the blame, for he has sinned and now he shall be punished.

Jacob picks up his chalk and gets to work.

❧ 65 ❧

CORNELIS

Life is half spent before we know what it is.

Jacob Cats, *Moral Emblems*, 1632

It it is midnight by the time Cornelis arrives home. He closes the door and stands in the front room. Maria has left the oil lamp burning. Its light glows on the blind wooden panels hanging on the wall. His paintings have turned their beautiful faces away so that they cannot see what is happening. Art creates a world of peace; the bloodiest murders – the massacre of the innocents, Christ's crucifixion – they are distilled into beauty. The slaughtered John the Baptist cannot feel pain, for he is eternal and removed from the raw grief of those who have to continue living.

Cornelis looks at the cabinet of precious silverware, at the great rooms receding into the darkness. How greedily he has filled this place with treasures, but it is all an illusion. Sophia has realized this. She has given it all up for love and cast herself adrift. *Don't blame her for it*, said the boy. Cornelis does not blame her, not now. For if she can give it up, so can he.

Cornelis climbs the stairs. He can no longer remain in this house, the object of gossip and pity – no doubt of ridicule, too. He pulls a canvas bag out of the closet and starts packing. A weight has been lifted from him; he feels as light and free as the night, a hundred years ago, in another life, when he lost his faith. (*Last night; it was last night.*) He knows what he is going to do, now. Sophia is alive, She has been led astray by a man who is unworthy of her – the boy confirmed what Cornelis suspected all along. It was Jan who made her do it and he will pay for it with his life.

They're sailing at dawn ... There is no time to lose. Cornelis pulls the straps tight and carries the bag downstairs. He is travelling light. Upstairs, the closets groan with his clothes, the shed skins of his vanity. He has sloughed off the burden of years, he feels like a young man again. Sophia thinks that he is a boring old pedant. He will show her how wrong she is. He, too, is capable of an impulsive act, all in the name of love.

And nobody will punish him. This is his deepest secret, the secret that sets him free. For he, and he alone, knows that God does not exist. He, and he alone, will take responsibility for his actions. Cornelis has stepped into the modern world, a brave new era of human accountability. He walks past the Bible, lying open on the lectern, and closes it with a thud.

He makes his way down the steps into the kitchen. In the fireplace the embers still glow. The room smells of fried onions and tom-cat. He approaches the half-curtained bed and holds out the candle to look inside. Willem and Maria lie together, sleeping. The fish seller's rubbery lips are parted; he exhales hoarsely. Maria's breath whistles in her nostrils. Between their faces is a tuft of dark hair; their daughter slumbers between them.

Cornelis feels a stab of pain. How contented they look. He is an intruder on their happiness. They have their baby; for them, all is well. Cornelis's throat is dry; he can barely swallow. Already, before he has relinquished it, he is a stranger in his own home.

He leaves the note, and a banker's draft, on the kitchen table.

I am going overseas. It may be for a long time. If something should befall me and I do not return, I leave this house to you and your daughter, for in the eyes of the world she is my heir. It is only we ourselves who know the truth. Keep it close to your hearts.

Please settle this payment on behalf of my wife's family, for they are innocents in this affair. I wish you all happiness. Turn the paintings round and enjoy their beauty, for they shall outlast us all.

C. S.

The port never sleeps. It is ruled by the tides and they obey no clocks. Barrels are being unloaded from the fishing boats. Someone is whistling a tune Cornelis has not heard since he was a boy. A mongrel bitch, her dugs so heavy with milk that they drag on the ground, walks stiffly on bowed legs. *We must engage a wet-nurse.* How humiliatingly he has been duped. All his wealth and education, to be hoaxed by a simple servant girl. The world has indeed been turned upside-down.

Yet how sweetly they slumbered. His anger has disappeared; his resentment is all but gone. Maria has acted wickedly but Cornelis knows that no punishment awaits her; she can sleep soundly. In truth, the reunion with her sweetheart, the untangling of their misunderstanding, touched his heart. They will bring life back to those rooms; he feels like a woody old bush, old growth, cleared away to let in the sunshine.

New shoots will grow in his space.

Cornelis thinks: a daughter has drifted in and out of my life; one blink and she has gone.

He feels strangely exhilarated. In the darkness he recognizes faces – Samuel Solomon, the Jewish cotton merchant, who stands by the quay watching bales being unloaded; the blind beggar for whom day and night are meaningless. This port is Cornelis's home from home. The odour of the sea is in his nostrils; it is the smell of his wealth and of his working life. Like Willem, the ocean has delivered up his livelihood and now he will finally deliver up himself to her mercies. And when he has left, all this bustle will carry on as if he has never been a part of it at all.

The sky is flushed pink. Among the rigging he sees the tall masts of the *Empress of the East*. His wife and her lover will already be aboard. Cornelis has no compunction about killing Jan. It will take place when they have left land far behind; the waves will swallow up the evidence, for they have swallowed up worse secrets than this. Cornelis knows the captain well. The man's silence can be bought for twenty florins; for forty florins more he will arrange for the deed to be done. Besides, he owes Cornelis a favour.

And when Jan has gone to his watery grave Cornelis will reclaim his wife and they will sail to Batavia together and live on his nutmeg plantation. Despite everything, he still loves her – look, he has given up everything for her. She will learn to love him because he has changed; he is no longer the man she married, he himself can no longer recognize that man. Anything, now, is possible.

Life is short; time is fleeting. *Grasp it while you can*, said the painter. And for once Cornelis has to agree with him.

Cornelis takes one last look at his beloved city, pearly in the dawn. The fog has lifted, the fog of his befuddled past; a thrilling and terrible dawn has broken. The clear blue skies of reason await him, and a new life with the woman whom he reclaimed once and whom he will reclaim again.

He buys his passage and boards the ship. He is only just in time. A few minutes later she weighs anchor and sets sail for the East.

❧ 66 ❧

JAN

Symptoms of tulip virus: Patterns of yellow discoloration (mosaics, ringspots, mottles) are common. Cause: Sub-microscopic virus particles in the sap of infected plants may be transmitted to healthy tissues by sap-feeding pests such as aphids, by nematodes or other soil-borne pests.

Royal Horticultural Society, *Encyclopaedia of Gardening*

Early in 1637 the tulip market crashes. The High Court of Holland, appalled at the national hysteria, intervenes and overnight bulbs are declared worthless. Thousands of people are made destitute. They throw themselves into the canals; they deliver themselves up to the mercy of the charitable institutions; in churches throughout the land they bitterly repent their folly. This curious episode sinks back into the margin of history, an episode which testifies to man's greed and the fickleness of fate. Yet it all stems from a love of beauty, a passion for flowers whose lives are even briefer than those who are in thrall to them. The fact that the most valuable of these blooms – the most spectacular mutations – are produced by a viral disease will be an irony discovered only in future years. If the predicants had known at the time, what sermons would they have thundered from their pulpits!

When men woke from their dream the blooms had withered but the paintings remained. Lovers, when parted, find solace in a portrait of their beloved. In centuries to come people will find balm in a beauty that once caused such suffering.

And Jan van Loos, through pain, will find greatness. *You have to be courageous, my friend*, said Matthcus. *Only through pain will the beauty of the world be revealed.* After losing Sophia he becomes a recluse. He rents another studio in his old neighbourhood and devotes himself to his art. He specializes in *vanitas* paintings – canvases that show, through the humblest of objects, the transience of life. An onion – he often paints an onion – lies next to a sandglass, a broken bread roll, a skull. Food becomes a sacrament; a transcendental homeliness, like incense, infuses his work. Out of suffering he creates great art. And in many of his paintings there is a curved mirror, a wineglass or a silver jug. Reflected in these is not the painter, hard at work. It is a woman, in a cobalt-blue dress, with soft brown hair. Her mirrored image haunts his paintings but her identity will never be confirmed, though scholars will see a resemblance in the bold, passionate nudes of 1636, where the woman gazes with such candid love out of her frame.

She reappears in one of his masterpieces, now hanging in the Dresden Museum. It shows a still life: an onion lies on a porcelain plate, its papery skin half peeled. Cards and dice are scattered on the table-cloth and an open book reveals a page in Latin script: *We played, we gambled, we lost.*

In a vase is one tulip: white petals blushed with pink, like the flushed cheek of a woman who has just risen from her lover's bed. On a petal there is a dewdrop. The woman's image is reflected there. You need a magnifying glass to see her; she appears to be trembling . . . like a dewdrop, her time is short before she vanishes for ever.

67

MARIA

Little boats should keep the shore; larger ships may venture more.

Jacob Cats, *Moral Emblems*, 1632

Maria, in her past life, dreamt that she changed places with her mistress. She dressed up in her blue jacket, with the white fur trim, and paraded in front of her own reflection. At night she dreamt that her mistress was drowned and that she, Maria, inherited this great house on the Herengracht and swam with her children through its rooms.

Now her dreams have been realized. Others have died so that she can live. Sophia has been missing for six years now, presumed drowned. Mr Sandvoort never returned. In all but name the house now belongs to Maria. She has two children, both girls, and her husband Willem. It is 1642 and they are sitting for their portrait in the library with the chequer-board floor.

Through the coloured panes of glass the sun shines on Willem, in his black jacket and breeches, and on the ivory lustre of Maria's dress. Her daughters Sophia and Amelia sit, straight-backed, on chairs. Their King Charles spaniel lies at their feet. They too crave immortality and will hang in the Mauritshuis in The Hague: *Unknown Man, his Wife and Daughters by Jacob Haecht 1620–1675* (Signed and dated 1642). For Jacob has become a fashionable portrait painter, noted for the meticulous detail of his brushwork. He will never be a great master; he will not scale the heights of Jan van Loos, but he will please his public.

As he paints them, Jacob asks: 'What happened to the old man – Mr Sandvoort?'

'Who knows?' replies Willem. 'All we've heard are rumours.' News from the East Indies takes months to travel and is notoriously unreliable. 'Some say he died of the yellow fever.' Willem, who has put on weight and become a little pompous, flicks a speck of dust off his jacket.

'I don't believe it,' says Maria. 'I heard that he set up home with a beautiful native girl.'

'Who told you?' asks Willem.

'Just someone I met.' She pauses, relishing their attention. 'It's said that he still lives with her in sinful pleasure, for he has never solemnized their union – in fact, he has never set foot inside a church.'

'Is that true?' asks Willem.

'*I* believe it,' replies Maria. 'Doesn't he deserve some happiness?'

'Don't smile,' says Jacob. 'I'm painting your mouth.'

He paints for a while in silence. The girls shift in their chairs; their dresses rustle. The dog has fallen asleep.

'I painted him six years ago,' says Jacob. 'I painted most of him. Do you remember?'

Maria nods.

Jacob looks at the little girl. 'His daughter resembles him, do you not agree?'

Maria grins. 'You think so?' She bends down to stroke the little girl's hair. 'I don't.'

'Sit still please,' says Jacob sharply.

❦ 68 ❧

JAN

The days of man are but as grass: for he flourisheth as a flower of the field.

For as soon as the wind goeth over it, it is gone: and the place thereof shall know it no more.

Psalm 103

It is a blustery morning in September 1648, rinsed and shiny. Jan is walking to the market to buy some food. His kitchen is empty; he has been shut away in his studio, working like a man possessed, and has lost all track of time.

Emerging into the dazzling day he blinks in the sunshine. Stallholders flap their arms at scavenging dogs; hawkers shout their wares. A chestnut mare plants her hind legs apart, raises her tail and releases a torrent of streaming urine on to the cobblestones. How sturdily alive she looks! Her shiny haunches, damp with sweat; her flaring nostrils. She snorts, groaning with satisfaction, as she relieves herself. This is her life; there is no other. The horse is untroubled by fears of mortality. *Mankind's hopes are fragile glass and life is therefore also short.* Little does she care.

Jan himself has no fear of death. Twelve years earlier, when Sophia died, he too ceased living in this world. He closed that door and opened another, a world he creates in his paintings. This is his reality, the stillness of his still lifes, and when he steps outside it startles him to see people bustling to and fro, going about their business. It still surprises him, after so many years, that the world carries on so heedlessly without her. Babies are born; piles are driven into the mud of the Damplein for the erection of the great Town Hall of Amsterdam, which will be a monument to civic pride and a cause of wonderment in all who will behold it.

Sophia's life has been stilled but she still inhabits his heart. He talks to her and feels her holding her breath to listen. Her immortality lives within him and within his paintings, for he paints her reflection trapped in the curve of a glass. She has a life, still, in his still lifes. And he has no fear of death for he has survived what, at the time, felt like extinction. In fact, he will live to be sixty-one (*Jan van Loos 1600–1661*), the span of this Golden Age, and his greatest work has yet to be painted. On this windy day in September, however, he is simply struck by the sunlight on the metallic scales of the heaped-up herrings. How could they be dead when they gleam so brightly? Does it matter that they have died if, when an artist paints them, they will become alive again?

Jan stops at a stall and buys an apple. Later, he remembers this moment. He bites into the apple; the juice spurts. Nearby lie some spilled entrails; a crow stands there, one claw planted on them while it pulls the glistening guts with its beak. Jan is remembering when he was a boy, how he watched his father beating silver into shape, its brightness glinting in the murky workshop. He thinks of the twin sheens of fish and silver platter, and how he misses his father, who has been dead for many years.

As he munches the apple he is aware of grey shapes moving across the square. They move like shadows for they are nuns from the convent and have but a spectral existence, like a lost memory of their own lives, in this world. There is one Catholic convent in the centre of the city, a closed order impenetrable to outsiders. Behind its walls the nuns have delivered themselves up to God; they spend their days in prayer. When they emerge their faces are veiled in black.

One nun walks a little apart from the others. There is something familiar about the way she moves – her tallness, her hesitancy. In the wind, her habit billows about her slender body.

He gazes at her. She is separated from him by the milling shoppers. She stops dead. She stands transfixed, like a startled deer, her hand gripping the crucifix that hangs around her neck.

At that moment the wind blows the veil from her face. Just a glimpse – that is all. Then she veers away and slips through the crowd.

Jan stands there, frozen. A hand is thrust in front of his face. 'May the Lord have mercy on your soul.'

Jan fumbles in his purse. Can he believe his eyes? Does she live still; could it be possible? Or has dreaming her into life, into paint, so possessed him that he can no longer separate art from illusion?

While scrabbling for coins Jan's attention is distracted. When he looks up the nun is gone. This grey, hooded figure – a ghost, in her final disguise – she has disappeared, as if she is simply a figment of his imagination.

ACKNOWLEDGEMENTS

For their comments and help, my thanks to
Manouk van der Meulen, Russell Hoban,
Wolfgang Ansorge, Judy Cooke, Geraldine Cooke,
Patricia Brent, Periwinkle Unwin, Victoria Salmon,
Jacques Giele, Lee Langley, Sarah Garland,
Alex Hough, Anne Rothenstein, Judy Taylor,
Charlotte Ackroyd, Geraldine Willson-Fraser,
Lottie Moggach, Tom Moggach, and Csaba Pasztor.
The many books I found useful and illuminating
included Simon Schama's *The Embarrassment of Riches*,
Paul Zumthor's *Daily Life in Rembrandt's Holland*,
Mariet Westerman's *A Worldly Art*,
Wayne E. Franit's *Paragons of Virtue*, Bob Haak's
The Golden Age, R. H. Fuchs's *Dutch Painting*,
Michael North's *Art and Commerce in the Dutch Golden
Age*, Paul Taylor's *Dutch Flower Painting 1600–1750* and
Z. Herbert's *Still Life with a Bridle*.

Most of all, my thanks to the Dutch artists themselves,
through whose paintings we step into a lost world,
and find ourselves at home.

LIST OF ILLUSTRATIONS